The Vengeance Trail

After saloon girl Kitty O'Hara shoots Billy Tranter in self-defence, she flees town in terror of the consequences and heads north out of Texas.

Kitty is pursued by Billy's elder brother, Captain Johnnie Tranter of the Texas Rangers, who is determined to exact revenge for Billy's death. Johnnie's plans are thwarted, however, when Wolf Brennan's gang hold up Kitty's stagecoach and she escapes with the outlaws.

Meanwhile, the famous Kentuckian gunfighter, Jack Stone, is on the case. It might take all of his courage and resourcefulness to bring the matter to a satisfactory conclusion . . . but they don't come tougher or deadlier than Jack Stone.

The Vengeance Trail

J.D. Kincaid

A Black Horse Western

ROBERT HALE · LONDON

© J.D. Kincaid 2010
First published in Great Britain 2010

ISBN 978-0-7090-8961-2

Robert Hale Limited
Clerkenwell House
Clerkenwell Green
London EC1R 0HT

www.halebooks.com

Typeset by
Derek Doyle & Associates, Shaw Heath
Printed and bound in Great Britain by
CPI Antony Rowe, Chippenham and Eastbourne

ONE

It was high noon and a warm April sun shone down upon the small Texas cattle town of Double Drop, as Billy Tranter rode down Main Street and pulled up in front of the Longhorn Saloon. He dismounted, hitched his sorrel gelding to the rail, trotted up the short flight of wooden steps leading on to the sidewalk, pushed open the batwing doors and stepped inside.

Billy was the younger son and third child of Colonel John Tranter, owner of a thriving horse ranch situated a couple of miles outside the town. The colonel was also the town's deputy mayor and one of the wealthiest men in Maxwell County. His elder son, Johnnie, had enlisted in the Texas Rangers and, much to the colonel's and his wife Mary's delight, had swiftly risen to the rank of captain. The colonel's second child, Ruth, had also done well in

5

her parents' eyes, having made a good match with a neighbouring rancher, one even wealthier than the colonel. Only Billy had disappointed. Spoiled from an early age, he had shown a disinclination to make anything of himself. Lazy and shiftless, Billy was supposed to help his father run the horse ranch, but did little or no work and spent most of his time in Double Drop, where he drank to excess, gambled and fornicated with the Longhorn Saloon's sporting women. He also had a quick temper and was frequently involved in drunken brawls. Indeed, only the colonel's influence had, so far, kept him out of jail.

A stranger would never have guessed that Billy Tranter was such a disreputable character, however, for he was a tall, broad-shouldered young man of twenty-three, with a head of thick blond hair, a handsome, open countenance, a pair of bright blue eyes and a ready smile. Moreover, he was invariably presentably attired in a neat, low-crowned black Stetson, a freshly laundered white shirt, an expensive brown suede jacket, black denim pants and highly-polished black leather boots. He carried a Colt Peacemaker in a brown leather holster tied down on his right thigh and a razor-sharp hunting knife in a sheath at his waist. Such was the young man who, that afternoon, made his way across the bar room floor towards the bar with its hammered copper top.

'Afternoon, Billy,' said Sam Hood the proprietor, a small, stocky man in a white shirt and black vest, and wearing a rather grubby white apron over his trousers.

'Hi, Sam,' responded Billy amiably.

'The usual?'

'Yup.'

Sam Hood poured the youngster a hefty measure of red-eye. Billy smiled and threw back the whiskey in one gulp. He slapped the glass down on to the copper bar top.

'Same again?' asked the saloonkeeper.

'You got it, Sam,' replied Billy.

As he consumed the second whiskey at a rather more leisurely pace, Billy glanced round the bar room. There was the usual mixture of customers at the bar: townsfolk, homesteaders and cowboys, and, arguing at one end of it, two of the town drunks, Tubby Jinks and Freddie Blake. Of the saloon's sporting women only one was in view, the others being either off duty or upstairs with a client. The Longhorn's poker school occupied a large table in the centre of the saloon. Billy noted that there were half a dozen players. He grinned and finished the second whiskey.

'Fill it up, Sam,' he said, pushing the empty glass across the counter towards the saloonkeeper.

Sam Hood did as he was bid and then, looking the

youngster straight in the eye, asked for payment.

Billy Tranter scowled, but dug his hand into his pocket and pulled out a wad of banknotes. He peeled off a couple of five-dollar bills and slapped them down on the counter.

'I'm gonna play me a li'l poker,' he drawled. 'Jest keep the whiskeys comin', will you?'

'Of course, Billy. My pleasure,' said Hood, as he deftly scooped up the two banknotes.

Billy picked up his drink and sauntered across the bar room towards the poker table.

'Mind if I join you gents?' he enquired.

'No. Pull up a chair,' replied Silas Charnley amiably.

Charnley was the town's one and only lawyer. He was also an extremely astute card-player. He was a tall, lean, hawk-faced man, invariably attired in an expensive three-piece, city-style suit, and he maintained an impassive countenance at all times. Consequently, it was impossible to tell whether he held a good hand or was bluffing. Billy Tranter, on the other hand, often betrayed the quality of his hand by either a smile or a scowl. He couldn't stop himself and, therefore, rarely left the card table a winner.

That afternoon, however, the cards initially fell kindly for Billy and, for the first two hours, he won steadily. It was then that he became rather too cocky and began to overplay his hands. The large pile of winnings, which Billy had placed before him on the table, rapidly diminished. Soon it was all gone and he was forced to pull from his pocket his remaining banknotes.

In a vain attempt to retrieve his losses, Billy gambled ever more recklessly. But Lady Luck had deserted him. In one last desperate fling, he bet the last of his money on a pair of deuces. His bluff failed and he was cleaned out. He gulped down the whiskey, which one of Sam Hood's bartenders had placed in front of him, and glanced beseechingly across the room towards the bar. The saloonkeeper stared back and shook his head. Billy Tranter's whiskey-money had run out.

'I don't s'pose you fellers would allow me a li'l credit?' he murmured hopefully.

Silas Charnley shrugged his shoulders.

'You know the rules, Billy,' said the lawyer. 'This game is played for cash only. You don't have the spondulicks, you don't play.'

'But, Hell, I'm good for—'

'No, Billy,' stated Charnley.

'Surely you—?'

Billy left the question unspoken. He could see, from the looks on the faces of the other poker players, that the rules were not about to be bent. He was clearly out of the game. Cursing, he pushed his chair back and got to his feet. Then he turned on his heel and stomped across the saloon towards the bar. He made no attempt to wheedle a free whiskey out of Sam Hood, but instead made for the saloon's only visible sporting woman.

Kitty O'Hara would not have been Billy's first choice. He preferred the other, younger saloon girls. Kitty was a redhead in her late thirties and, although still very attractive, the signs of ageing were just beginning to show: a few tell-tale lines on the face and neck, a slight thickening round the waist. But her green eyes were as bright and inviting as ever, her wide, sensuous mouth bore a saucy smile, her full, ripe breasts were provocatively displayed in a low-cut, dark-green satin gown and her slender, shapely legs were shown to advantage due to the gown's hip-to-ankle slit. A tumble with the redhead would, Billy felt, take his mind off his losses at the poker table.

He slipped his arm round her waist and said, 'Hows about you an' me headin' upstairs?'

Kitty favoured him with her professional smile. That Billy was as handsome as any young man in the county Kitty didn't dispute. Yet the other saloon girls did not care for him. He could be very rough, even cruel, and he left them in no doubt that he thoroughly despised them. Still, there were several clients whom Kitty and the others disliked, but were nevertheless obliged to entertain. Consequently, she in turn slipped her arm round Billy's waist murmured in a husky voice, 'Sure thing, honey.

She had been paying little or no attention to poker game and, so, did not realize that Billy had l all of his money at the table. Sam Hood had guess at Billy's financial situation, but, unfortunately, wa busy serving a customer when the couple set ou towards the flight of stairs leading to the saloon's upper floor. They were disappearing across the upstairs balcony and down the narrow passage, along which were located the saloon's various bedrooms, when suddenly he observed them. However, it was too late to warn Kitty. Hood shrugged his shoulders. Kitty knew his rule. She would have to explain it to Billy. He just hoped there would be no trouble.

Upstairs, Kitty opened the door of her bedroom and stepped inside. Billy Tranter followed, By this time, the youngster's passions were fully roused and he could scarcely contain himself. He plunged a hand into the cleavage of the redhead's dress and grasped hold of one of her firm white breasts, while, with the other, he ripped the dark-green dress off her body and hurled it to one side. Straightaway, Kitty pushed him hard in the chest and tore herself free from his grasp. In so doing, she staggered a few feet backwards and came up against the foot of the bed.

'What ... what do you think you're doin'?' she cried.

and

the

st

d

s

I'm doin'?' he retorted, as he

black denim pants.

rst!' she protested.

manded Billy.

the house. You don't pay, you don't

virtually what Silas Charnley had said to
poker table. Billy's face reddened, his eyes
angrily and he snarled, 'You don't tell me
an an' cannot do, you goddam whore!'

Hood, he don't allow—' the redhead began,
a full-bodied slap across the face silenced her
sent her sprawling backwards on to the bed.

As Billy dived on top of her, Kitty swiftly brought
up her knee and caught him in the testicles. Billy let
out an anguished yell and clutched the injured parts.
He subsided on to the bottom half of the bed, where
for a few moments he crouched doubled over,
gasping heavily and evidently in some considerable
pain. During the short period of respite which this
gained her, Kitty half-turned in the bed and slipped
her right hand beneath the pillow.

Swearing roundly, Billy slowly pulled himself up
on to his knees. Then he leaned down over the side
of the bed and pulled the razor-sharp hunting knife
from the sheath fixed to the belt around his
discarded denim pants. He brandished this weapon
and crawled across the bed towards the redhead.

'I'm gonna cut you up real good,' he hissed, his eyes glinting malevolently.

Then, as he suddenly thrust himself at her, Kitty pulled out the two-barrelled derringer, which she kept hidden beneath her pillow for just such an emergency. (Sam Hood had advised all of his sporting women to take this precaution.) And, with the point of the hunting knife pricking her throat, the redhead squeezed the trigger. Once. Twice. Both barrels were pressed hard against Billy's torso when Kitty fired. As a result, the sound of the shots was largely muffled, while their force lifted Billy clean off the redhead. An expression of blank surprise suffused his countenance, and then he gasped and promptly collapsed. As he did so, Kitty hastily squirmed to one side and slipped off the bed. She hit the floor in the same instant that Billy sprawled face down on to the mattress.

It took a few seconds before Kitty could recover her wits. Thereupon, she slowly, nervously, clambered to her feet and stared down at the figure spreadeagled across the bed. Billy's face lay sideways on the pillow, the one visible eye staring sightlessly at the far wall. There was no question that he was dead. She had killed him! Anxiously, she listened for the sound of approaching footsteps. Surely somebody in the bar room downstairs had heard those two shots? But no one came.

Not only had Billy Tranter's body helped muffle the sound of the shots, but, fortunately for Kitty, at the very moment she squeezed the trigger, a fracas had broken out in the bar room. The argument between the two drunks, Tubby Jinks and Freddie Blake, had finally developed into a full-scale brawl, which Sam Hood and his two bartenders had rushed to break up. In the ensuing struggle, several tables and chairs had been overturned, before, eventually, the two drunken combatants had been ejected. It was little wonder, then, that the shooting of Billy Tranter had passed unnoticed by both the staff and the customers of the Longhorn Saloon.

Kitty stood naked and trembling, the derringer still clutched in her hand. She glanced down again at the corpse on the bed. The razor-sharp hunting knife remained in Billy's grasp. Kitty felt her neck where the knife had pricked her. There was blood on her fingers. The blade had pierced her skin. She studied herself in the fly-blown mirror on her dressing-table. There was the merest pin-prick on her lily-white neck. She took a small lace handkerchief from her reticule, dabbed the spot and thanked her lucky stars. Had she delayed shooting for just half a second, the blade would surely have been thrust deep into her throat, severing her windpipe. Hers had undeniably been an act of self-defence.

But would a jury see it that way? That was the

14

question. The man she had killed was the son of Colonel James Tranter, a person of considerable influence within the county, while she was merely a common saloon girl. Therefore, would the actual evidence be ignored by the jury? Would they simply bow down to the pressure which the colonel was almost certain to exert, and find her guilty? It all depended upon the composition of the jury. And Kitty had no way of knowing who would be called upon to judge her.

The redhead made her mind up in an instant. Although innocent of Billy's murder, nevertheless there was a fair chance that she would be deemed guilty and hanged. She decided not to put the matter to the test. She would flee Double Drop forthwith.

Accordingly, Kitty dropped the derringer into her reticule and threw open the door of her wardrobe. Each of Sam Hood's sporting women had her own bedchamber, where she entertained her customers and where she slept and kept her belongings. Kitty was no exception and hanging inside the wardrobe were another dark-green dress, which fell in full flare to her ankles, a short cape and a bonnet in the same colour. Quickly, Kitty donned these articles of clothing and began to pack a small carpet-bag with her meagre supply of blouses, stockings and undergarments. Then she leant inside the wardrobe and removed what was a false bottom. From the recess thus revealed, Kitty proceeded to pick up the small amount of money she had accumulated over the years. At least, she thought to herself, she would not be destitute when she left town.

With the reticule hooked over her arm and the carpet-bag firmly grasped in one hand, Kitty stepped outside the room. She cast one last glance towards the body lying spreadeagled across the narrow bed, then quietly closed the door and set off down the passage. She did not, however, retrace her earlier steps, but headed in the opposite direction, towards the stairs at the rear of the saloon. These led down to a yard, where Sam Hood left his empty beer barrels and crates of whiskey bottles for collection. Kitty wended her way past the beer barrels and into an alley, which ran between Hood's Longhorn Saloon and Larry Gordon's general store. She hurried up this alley and out on to Main Street.

On the opposite side of the bustling thoroughfare stood the stage-line depot and, before it, the coach bound for Dallas. This stage, Kitty knew, was due to depart at three o'clock, as it did every afternoon. She turned and accosted a tall, thin, ginger-haired man in his early fifties, who happened to be strolling along the sidewalk in the direction of the barbering parlour. He was Nathaniel Parkins, the town's tailor and one of Kitty's regular customers.

'Afternoon, Nat,' she said. 'Can you tell me what time it is?'

'Time I had another tumble with you,' he replied jokingly.

'Oh, be serious, Nat!' remonstrated the redhead.

'Wa'al, Kitty, it's exactly five minutes 'fore three,' said the tailor, upon consulting the small fob watch, which he carried in his vest pocket.

'Thank you, Nat.'

'Are ... are you goin' somewhere?' enquired Parkins, eyeing her carpet-bag curiously.

'I'm aimin' to visit my sister for a few days,' she improvized.

'I'll see you when you git back,' said Parkins, grinning. 'Then, mebbe we'll have that tumble together.'

'You can bet on it,' lied Kitty.

The tailor doffed his hat and continued on his way down Main Street, while the redhead promptly crossed it and dived into the office of the stage-line depot, where she purchased a ticket, thereby securing herself a place on the afternoon stage.

Moments later, after the guard had hefted her carpet-bag up on to the roof and Kitty had taken the one remaining inside seat, the driver flicked the reins and set the stagecoach in motion. It rattled off along Main Street to take the trail northwards, via Cactus City, to its ultimate destination, Dallas. From there the redhead intended catching a train north to Kansas City.

Her hasty departure from Double Drop had given her no time to make proper plans. Kitty had focused only on escaping from the town before she was arrested for the killing of Billy Tranter. Well, she reasoned, she would have plenty of time to finalize her plans on the long train journey from Dallas to Kansas City. From Kansas City she could continue by train in a north-easterly direction to Chicago, or branch off further east to one of the large seaboard cities, New York perhaps, or Boston, where nobody, she felt sure, would find her.

As the stage crossed the town limits and headed out across the prairie, Kitty breathed a sigh of relief and began to relax.

However, she had not left Double Drop unnoticed. And it was not only Nathaniel Parkins who was aware of her departure. Directly opposite the stage-line office stood the law office, and outside it, on the sidewalk, Sheriff Joe Dunn sat in his rocking-chair, smoking a large, fat cigar and quietly observing the comings and goings up and down Main Street. He had earlier watched Tubby Jinks and Freddie Blake being ejected from the Longhorn Saloon. Since he didn't want the bother of locking them up, the sheriff had been relieved when they picked themselves up and, instead of resuming their brawl, staggered off in opposite directions. Then he had watched with interest as Kitty O'Hara clambered aboard the stage and it set off on its journey north.

Joe Dunn had been Maxwell County's sheriff for a little over twenty years. He was a slim-built, lean-faced man in his late forties, grey-haired and slow to anger. He carried a Colt Peacemaker, but these days rarely had the need to draw it. Over the years, he and his deputies had succeeded in establishing law and order in both the town of Double Drop and the surrounding county. Now his job was relatively easy and he felt entirely comfortable in his position of chief peace officer.

Sheriff Dunn continued to gaze after the stagecoach until, presently, it vanished from sight. He was puzzled. Kitty had been one of Sam Hood's sporting women for a number of years. Indeed, she was not only the oldest, but was also the longest-serving. It struck him as odd, therefore, that she should be leaving town. He had come to regard her as a fixture. He smiled wryly. Most women in her profession did move on. So, why should he be surprised? He took another puff at his cigar and resumed his observations of the town's comings and goings.

TWO

A quarter of an hour after the departure of the stage, Captain Johnnie Tranter of the Texas Rangers rode on to his parents' horse ranch. He was an older version of Billy. He had the same thick blond hair, a similar handsome, open countenance, and the same bright blue eyes and ready smile. No one who had seen the two could have taken them for anything other than brothers.

But Johnnie Tranter was seven years Billy's senior and rather less heavily built, although of about the same height as his brother. Also, he was both upright and dutiful, whereas Billy had been wild and feckless. Like Billy, he was smartly dressed. A black Stetson, black kerchief, crisp white shirt, black leather vest, denim pants and leather boots comprised his attire. Again, like Billy, he carried a Colt Peacemaker. And he rode a fine black stallion, a Winchester stuck in his saddleboot. His dress and selection of weapons were his own, for the Texas Rangers had no formal uniform. As a force, they were engaged in generally keeping the peace in the Lone Star State, and in tracking down horse thieves and cattle rustlers. They were reputed to 'ride like Mexicans, shoot like Tennesseeans, and fight like the very devil'.

Johnnie Tranter found his mother sitting on a rocking-chair on the veranda of the ranch house. He quickly dismounted, then bounded up the steps on to the veranda, where he greeted, embraced and kissed her.

'You received your father's message, then?' said Mary Tranter.

'I did, an' I set out straightaway,' replied Johnnie.

'Your father and I were sorry to summon you home so suddenly. It's a darned long ride from Austin.'

Johnnie shrugged his shoulders and smiled.

'Aw, it ain't so very far!' he demurred. He glanced round at the corrals and various outbuildings. 'But where is Papa?' he enquired.

As he spoke, Colonel James Tranter rounded the corner of the ranch house on his way back from the stables, where he had been giving instructions to two of his grooms.

The colonel, clad all in white, cut an impressive figure, with his mane of dark, grey-flecked hair and his haughty, aristocratic features. Ironically, the colonel's sons had both taken after their blonde mother, while it was his daughter Ruth who had inherited his dark, patrician looks.

'Ah, there you are, my boy!' he cried delightedly.

The two men embraced and then all three retired inside the ranch house. There, in a fine Colonial-style sitting-room, Mary Tranter rang for home-made lemonade and cakes. Then, once these had been brought and the servants had retired, Johnnie broached the reason for his visit.

'I had jest returned from a sortie against the Comanche when your wire arrived at headquarters. You said that my presence was required urgently, but you gave me no inkling as to why you needed to see me.'

'No, I felt it best not to,' said Colonel Tranter. 'It is, after all, a family matter an' not something I want others privy to.'

Johnnie smiled wryly.

'It's got to do with Billy, hasn't it?' he surmised.

'It has,' said the colonel heavily.

'We have, I fear, rather spoiled him,' confessed Mary Tranter.

Johnnie nodded.

'I'm afraid you have,' he agreed. 'Billy has had too much of his own way for too long.'

Colonel Tranter pulled a long face.

'Yes,' he said. 'It has been my fault. I've been much

22

too lenient. It's ironic really. As an old soldier, used to imposing discipline, I should surely have been able to control Billy. But I signally failed to do so.'

'You did try, James,' protested his wife.

'Though not hard enough,' said the colonel, shaking his head sadly.

'The result being that Billy has failed to settle down to anything and has become notorious in town for getting drunk and causing trouble. If it had not been for the affection in which your father is held, Billy would certainly have found himself in jail by now,' declared Mary.

'A disgrace which I refuse to contemplate,' said the colonel.

Johnnie frowned.

'So, you want me to take a hand in disciplinin' him,' he said.

'In a way,' said his father. 'I came to the conclusion that perhaps a spell in the Army would do him some good. But Billy refused point-blank to enlist, even though I threatened to cut him off without one red cent to his name.'

'However, he did say he would be prepared to enlist in the Texas Rangers,' said Mary. 'I think your father's threat and Billy's regard for you combined to prompt him into making this offer.'

'It could be jest what he needs,' said the colonel hopefully.

'Hmm, I s'pose it could,' agreed Johnnie, though without much conviction.

He had reservations about his younger brother becoming a Texas Ranger. But he had to admit that Billy was a good horseman and an excellent shot, and that he did not lack courage. Perhaps it would work?

'This is why I sent for you,' explained his father. 'Matters were rapidly getting out of hand. It was urgent that Billy be brought to heel. So, my boy, that's your task. I want you to escort Billy to your headquarters in Austin and, once there, get him to enlist, as he said he would.'

'OK. So, where is Billy?' asked Johnnie.

'Hmm. There's the rub,' said Colonel Tranter. 'I'm afraid he's gone into town.'

'Like he does most days,' added Mary.

'When did he go?'

'Jest 'fore noon,' said the colonel.

'Consequently, he could be drunk by now?'

'He could. Do you want to wait here at the ranch until he returns?'

'No, Papa. I'll go find him an' bring him back. If he *is* drunk, we'll needs wait until he sobers up 'fore we set out. But if he ain't, then we'll jest call in, say our farewells an' hit the trail.'

'OK, Johnnie. Thank you.'

The Texas Ranger embraced both his parents, then mounted the black stallion and set off to cover the two miles to Double Drop.

When he reached the town, Johnnie cantered down Main Street until he reached the Longhorn Saloon. This was where he expected to find his brother. He dismounted, hitched his horse to the rail outside and hurriedly entered the saloon.

Like his brother before him, he wended his way between the tables and across the bar room towards the bar. Then he observed the poker school and veered off towards the card table. The players had just completed a hand and Larry Gordon, the proprietor of Double Drop's general store, was in the process of gathering in his winnings. He glanced up as the young Texas Ranger approached the table.

'Afternoon, Johnnie. Nice to see you back in town,' he said amiably.

'Nice to be back,' replied Johnnie. 'You seen my brother, Billy? I figured I might find him with you fellers, playin' poker.'

'He was playin' earlier,' said Larry Gordon. 'But he ran outa luck.'

'An' cash,' added the lawyer, Silas Charnley, drily.

'I see. So he quit?'

'He was forced to. No credit extended,' said Charnley.

'That's the rule,' added Gordon.

'OK. Thanks. I'll leave you fellers to your game.'

'Yeah. 'Bye, Johnnie.'

' 'Bye.'

Johnnie continued on his way across the bar-room towards the bar, where he was greeted by Sam Hood.

'Hi there, Johnnie. Good to see you. What can I git you?' enquired the saloon-keeper.

'Nuthin' for the moment, Sam. I'm lookin' for Billy.'

'He went upstairs with Kitty.'

Johnnie nodded. While he had not personally enjoyed the favours of the Longhorn's sporting women, he was well aware that his younger brother often did so. 'How long since they went upstairs?' he asked.

' 'Bout half an hour, I reckon,' said Hood.

'They should be back down any time soon, then,' stated Johnnie.

'Yeah, though I'm kinda surprised they're still up there,' said Hood. 'Y'see, Billy's had hisself a fair few whiskies an', while alcohol may stimulate the desire, it sure don't aid the performance none.'

'No.' Johnnie observed the concerned look that had suddenly appeared in the saloon-keeper's eyes. Anxious to discover what was troubling him, he asked, 'Somethin' the matter, Sam?'

'Wa'al, the rule of the house is that, if'n you wanta tumble one of my gals, you gotta pay first.'

'No credit?'

'None given. Ever.'

'Kitty wouldn't have made an exception jest this once? Seein' as Billy is kinda regular.'

'No, I don't think so. She knows how strict I am on that point.'

'But Billy had lost all his money at the poker table. So, why in tarnation are they still upstairs?'

'That's what I'm wonderin', Johnnie.' Sam Hood gestured towards the crowd round the bar. 'I've been kinda busy. Otherwise I'd've gone to investigate,' he explained.

'Then let's go now,' said Johnnie urgently.

'OK.'

Leaving the bar in the care of his two bartenders, Hood raised a hatch and slipped through to the customers' side of the bar counter. Then, closely followed by Johnnie, he headed for the stairs leading to the upper floor. The two men mounted these in a few quick strides, crossed the upstairs balcony and stared down the narrow passage into which Billy and the redhead had earlier vanished.

'OK, Sam. Which bedroom's Kitty's?' demanded the Texas Ranger.

'The second on the left.'

Johnnie pushed past the saloon-keeper and hurried along the passage until he reached the room which Sam Hood had indicated. He paused for a moment outside and tapped loudly on the door.

There was no response.

'You in there, Billy?' he cried.

There was still no response.

'I'm comin' in, Billy!' yelled Johnnie, and he threw open the door and dashed into the room.

The sight of his brother, lying spreadeagled upon the bed with blood oozing from beneath his chest and across the bed sheets, caused the young man to halt in mid-stride and exclaim, 'Holy cow! Billy! Billy! God, the bitch has killed you!'

Sam Hood stared down at the corpse, the colour slowly draining from his face. The shock he suffered did not, however, prevent the saloon-keeper from observing the knife still clutched in Billy Tranter's right hand.

'Looks like Billy tried to knife Kitty an' she shot him in self-defence,' he muttered, as he continued to take in the scene in front of him.

'How'd you figure that out?' rasped Johnnie.

'Wa'al, it's the most likely explanation,' declared Hood.

'Is that so? Then why has the girl vamoosed, if'n it was self-defence an' not murder?' demanded Johnnie.

'I dunno. But what do you think happened?'

'I reckon it's more likely she pulled a gun on Billy an' that *he* drew the knife in self-defence. Only she shot him 'fore he could git to her.'

'Aw, come on, Johnnie!'

'That's how I see it,' reiterated Johnnie Tranter obstinately.

And that was exactly how he saw it, for he had deliberately shut out of his mind the terrible alternative. Billy was his kid brother and he could not, would not, believe that his kid brother was capable of murder. His explanation had to be the right one. Billy must surely have acted in self-defence.

'I'd best fetch the sheriff,' said Hood quietly.

'Yeah. You do that, Sam.'

'You comin' with me?'

'No, I'll wait here.'

'OK. Jest don't touch nuthin'.'

'I won't.'

Johnnie waited until the saloon-keeper had left the room. Then he stepped across to the bed and prised the knife from Billy's grasp. He replaced it in its sheath. He told himself that, by so doing, he was simply ensuring that Billy would be declared innocent; that, by removing the one piece of evidence which might suggest the contrary, he was preventing a possible miscarriage of justice. Such was the warped state of mind into which his brother's death had thrown him. Indeed, he had but two thoughts in his head. One, that Billy must be shown beyond all doubt to be the innocent victim, and two, that Billy's killer must pay for his death with her life.

The whore could not be permitted to kill his kid brother and get away with it.

He was kneeling by the side of the bed, his head bowed in prayer, when Sam Hood returned, accompanied by Sheriff Joe Dunn. He broke off from his prayers and looked up as the two men approached the bed.

'Howdy, Sheriff,' he said.

'Hi, Johnnie.' The sheriff gestured towards Billy Tranter's corpse. 'This is a darned bad business,' he commented.

'Sure is.'

'From what Sam says, it seems Kitty O'Hara shot your brother.'

'That's right. An' I'm expectin' you to arrest her an' charge her with his murder.'

'Wa'al, I dunno 'bout that.'

'Whaddya mean, Sheriff? It's your duty.'

'I know my duty, Johnnie. But, from what Sam says, it would appear that Kitty shot your brother in self-defence.'

'That's a goddam lie.'

'Wa'al, the knife in his—' Joe Dunn paused abruptly in mid-sentence and turned towards the saloon-keeper. 'Sam, you told me Billy was holdin' a knife,' he growled.

'So he was,' replied Hood.

'He ain't now.'

30

'He was when we found him.' Hood glanced down at the dead man's denim pants lying crumpled on the floor. Straightaway, he saw that the hunting knife had been returned to its sheath. 'That knife wasn't in its sheath then,' he stated emphatically.

'Oh, yes it was!' retorted Johnnie.

Sheriff Joe Dunn glanced bemusedly from one man to the other.

'One of you has gotta be lyin',' he rasped.

'Why in blue blazes should I lie?' demanded Hood.

' 'Cause Kitty is one of your sportin' women an' you're hell-bent on protectin' her,' said the young Texas Ranger.

'I ain't lyin', an' you know I ain't lyin', Johnnie. You took that thar knife outa Billy's hand an' stuck it back into its sheath, didn't you?'

'Nope.'

Johnnie Tranter remained deadpan. It was his word against the saloon-keeper's. And nobody could prove it was he, rather than Sam Hood, who was lying.

'You gonna take the word of a saloon-keeper, or that of a captain in the Texas Rangers?' Johnnie demanded of the sheriff.

Joe Dunn scratched his head.

'Wa-al. . . .' he began.

'You arrest Kitty O'Hara an' charge her with Billy's

murder. Then it's up to a jury to weigh the evidence an' come to a verdict.'

'Yeah. I guess so, Johnnie.'

The sheriff was pretty sure that Johnnie Tranter *had* tampered with the evidence, but he was loath to say as much. After all, he had no wish to antagonize Johnnie and, by the same token, Johnnie's father. Colonel James Tranter would be a bad man to have as an enemy. And Joe Dunn was due to stand for re-election in the following November. It was pretty much a foregone conclusion that he would easily see off any rivals. However, if the colonel were to back someone else. . . .

'So, what are you gonna do, Sheriff?' enquired the Texas Ranger.

'All right, Johnnie,' said Dunn. 'I'll issue a warrant for Kitty's arrest an'—'

'You cain't be serious!' exclaimed Sam Hood. 'Sure Kitty is a feisty, no-nonsense kinda young woman, but she ain't no murderess.'

'Like Johnnie said, that's for a jury to decide.'

'You said you'd issue a warrant for her arrest,' interjected Johnnie. 'Why don't you jest go an' arrest her? Why'd you need a warrant?'

' 'Cause she's left town,' said the sheriff.

'Whaddya mean, she's left town?'

'I saw her board the three o'clock stage, bound for Dallas.'

'Jeez!'

'Don't worry, Johnnie. I'll wire through to the next stop, that'll be Cactus City, an' git the marshal there to hold her till I can send one of my deppities over to fetch her back.'

'What time is it now?'

The sheriff glanced at Sam Hood, who extracted a large fob watch from his vest pocket.

'Almost exactly four o'clock,' stated the saloon-keeper.

'An hour behind. Hmm. I figure I can overtake the stage 'fore it reaches Cactus City,' declared Johnnie.

'Mebbe?' said the sheriff doubtfully.

'Certainly 'fore it leaves again. There'll be a change of horses an'. . . .'

'Why bother, Johnnie? Jest let me take care of this. Marshal Luther Grey is a good man. He'll be sure to grab Kitty off the stage an' hold her till my deppity gits there.'

'No. Billy's my brother. I'll go after her an' bring her back. There's no need for you to send a deppity.'

'Wa'al. . . .'

'Jest wire the marshal like you said, an' tell him to hold Kitty till I arrive. You can say you've deputized me to bring her back to Double Drop.'

Johnnie Tranter's tone brooked no argument. Sheriff Joe Dunn shrugged his shoulders. He didn't like it, yet he was simply not prepared to defy the young Texas Ranger.

'OK,' he said. 'I'll write out a warrant for you to present to Marshal Grey in Cactus City.'

'Thanks, Sheriff!' said Johnnie.

Sam Hood decided that he had best keep quiet. He felt that he had said enough already. If and when Kitty O'Hara was brought back to Double Drop to stand trial, he would needs give evidence. What would he say? Like the sheriff, he had no wish to provoke either Johnnie's or, more importantly, Colonel Tranter's enmity. Well, he mused, he would cross that bridge when he came to it.

Meantime, Johnnie was anxious to be gone.

'I've gotta git after that stage,' he said. 'So, Sheriff, can I leave it to you to inform my parents 'bout what's happened to Billy?'

' 'Course you can, Johnnie. I'll ride straight over an' give the colonel the bad news,' promised Joe Dunn.

'OK. Now write me out that warrant.'

'Sure thing.'

Leaving Sam Hood to contact the mortician, the other two headed for the law office, where the sheriff quickly did as he was bid and, when he was done, handed the paper to the Texas Ranger.

Johnnie scanned it briefly and nodded his satisfaction.

' 'Bye, Sheriff,' he said.

' 'Bye, Johnnie,' murmured Joe Dunn.

Johnnie Tranter hurriedly retraced his steps and soon found himself outside the saloon and unhitching his black stallion. He leapt into the saddle and set off along Main Street at a brisk canter. By the time he had left Double Drop and was heading northwards, Johnnie was riding at full gallop.

He had told Sheriff Dunn that he would bring Kitty O'Hara back to Double Drop, to stand trial for Billy's murder. But that was not his intention. While Kitty was afraid a jury might convict her, Johnnie feared that it would not. And he wasn't prepared to take the chance. Once he had the redhead in his clutches, he determined to act as judge, jury and executioner.

THREE

Wolf Brennan and his gang of outlaws occupied the bluff overlooking Coyote Gulch. It was four o'clock in the afternoon and they were expecting the stage bound for Dallas to hove into sight at any moment.

There were twelve men under Wolf Brennan's command: four white men, four half-breeds and four renegade Comanche Indians. Out of these were three, one from each group, whom Brennan had appointed as his lieutenants, namely Lo-Lo McCoy, Pawnee Pete and Blue Duck.

Wolf Brennan was aptly named. He was a tall, lean individual, with a livid white scar disfiguring the right side of his wolfish, unshaven face and cruel black eyes glittering out from above a large, hooked nose. He was dressed entirely in black: Stetson, shirt, leather jacket, Levis and boots, and he wore a Remington tied down on his right thigh, while he carried a Colt Hartford revolving rifle in his left hand.

Lo-Lo McCoy, in contrast, was short and stocky and heavily bearded. He had a mouthful of broken, brown-stained teeth and wore a sweat-soiled check shirt beneath his sheepskin coat. He, too, carried a Remington in his holster.

Pawnee Pete, the half-breed, was a veritable barrel of a man, with deep-set black eyes, high cheekbones, a flat nose and thick lips. His hair was held in place by a bright yellow bandana and he was dressed from head to toe in buckskin. He carried the inevitable Remington, together with a Bowie knife, the latter in a sheath at his waist.

Brennan's third lieutenant, Blue Duck, was a full-blooded Comanche brave, a tall, powerfully built young man with shoulder-length black hair and haughty, aquiline features. Like the half-breed, he was clad in buckskin, but, unlike the others, he favoured a Colt Peacemaker. There was also a Winchester in his saddleboot and his mount was a small, sturdy coal-black pony.

The rest of Wolf Brennan's gang were variously attired, some sporting jackets, some leather vests and others ankle-length leather coats, and all were armed with a mixture of Remingtons and Colt Peacemakers. Apart from their leader and Blue Duck, only three carried a rifle. All of them were mounted, ready to ride down into Coyote Gulch as soon as they spotted the stagecoach. After several unsuccessful months, during which they had operated as three separate gangs, they had met up and agreed to join forces under Wolf Brennan's leadership. The attack on the Dallas stage was to be their first venture together.

Wolf Brennan aimed his binoculars down the trail in the direction of Double Drop and in due time saw the cloud of dust kicked up by the coach and horses. He smiled grimly.

'OK, boys,' he rasped. 'Here she comes.'

'Let's git goin', then!' cried Lo-Lo McCoy.

'No,' said Brennan. 'Not yet. We wait till the stage turns round that last bend into the gulch. Then we ride down an' hold it up.'

And so, having masked their faces with their kerchiefs, the outlaws contained their impatience and waited.

Meantime, the driver of the stage, his shot-gun guard and their passengers continued on towards Coyote Gulch, blissfully unaware of the danger into which they were riding.

The six riding inside the stagecoach were a mixed bunch. Kitty O'Hara, in her dark-green dress, cape and bonnet, sat demurely in one corner of the stage. Next to her was Buddy Jones, a middle-aged, balding dry goods salesman, and next to him Ned Burns, a large, fat, jovial individual in his late thirties. He, too, was a salesman, hawking a famous Tennessee whiskey. Both men sported derby hats and three-piece, city-style suits, Jones favouring the colour grey and Burns a brown hat and a rather lurid check.

Opposite the two salesmen were the Reverend Frank Sanders and his wife, Annie. He was sombrely-clad and quite severe-looking, with a long, narrow face culminating in a lantern jaw, while his wife, a small, grey-haired woman, in contrast had a pleasant, placid countenance and warm brown eyes. Kitty had told Nathaniel Parkins that she was off to visit an imaginary sister. The clergyman and his wife were in fact travelling to Dallas for just such a purpose. They were intending to visit Annie's sick sister.

The sixth occupant of the stagecoach faced Kitty. Matt Lewis was a handsome young man, with penetrating blue eyes and a pugnacious, square-cut jaw-line. Dark-brown hair showed beneath his low-crowned black Stetson and his slim body was encased in a crisp white shirt, black vest and black Prince Albert coat. His trousers and shiny leather shoes were of the same hue, and he carried a pearl handled Colt revolver, the only one of the passengers except Kitty to be in possession of a weapon. He was an employee of the prestigious Pinkerton Detective Agency, with business to conduct in Dallas.

When Kitty had joined the others at Double Drop, a few pleasantries had been exchanged and she had discovered that all were aiming to dismount at the stage's final destination, Dallas. Indeed, the clergyman and his wife had engaged seats for the entire length of the stagecoach's journey, from San Antonio to Dallas. The others had boarded the stage at various points along its route.

The conversation inside the coach was maintained almost exclusively by the Reverend Frank Sanders and the two salesmen. Kitty's mind was too absorbed with recalling the killing of Billy Tranter and reviewing her current perilous situation. The possibility could not be discounted that Billy's corpse might be discovered and a pursuit initiated *before* she could reach and then leave Dallas for a new life up north. As for Annie Sanders, her thoughts were concentrated solely on the condition of her sick sister. And Matt Lewis also seemed disinclined to talk.

On the box, veteran driver Ollie Bailey and his equally experienced shot-gun guard Donnie Quick were pretty relaxed as the stagecoach entered Coyote Gulch. They had completed this journey dozens of times without incident. It was months, and indeed years, since the Dallas stage had been held up. Consequently, both men had grown a little complacent. Neither was as vigilant as he might have been.

The result was that Wolf Brennan and his band of

desperadoes took them entirely by surprise. Faced by the outlaws as they turned round a bend in the gulch, both men promptly went for their guns. Donnie Quick was the first to fire. His shot-gun blasted once, twice, and two of the bandits were toppled from their horses. But, in the next instant, a shot from Brennan struck him in the chest and knocked him clean off the box. At the same time, Lo-Lo McCoy shot Ollie Bailey between the eyes as the stagecoach driver attempted to draw his Colt Peacemaker. Then Brennan leapt aboard the careering coach, grabbed the reins from the dying driver and, with some difficulty, eventually succeeded in bringing the terrified horses and the stage to a shuddering halt.

As the stagecoach stopped, one of the doors flew open and Matt Lewis jumped out, his pearl-handled Colt in his hand. However, before he could bring it to bear on any of the outlaws, Blue Duck fired. The shot hit the Pinkerton agent in the right shoulder and sent him staggering backwards. As he fell, the revolver flew from his grasp, and he ended up flat on his back and quite defenceless.

'OK,' rasped Wolf Brennan, 'let's have no more heroics. The rest of you come outa that stage with your hands in the air.'

This command was reluctantly obeyed. Firstly, Kitty disembarked, her reticule in her hand; then the

Reverend Frank Sanders helped his tremulous wife to descend. He was quickly followed by Ned Burns, carrying a small case full of whiskey samples; and lastly by the dry goods salesman, Buddy Jones. All were pale-faced and visibly shaken. They huddled together in a small, anxious group.

'You, git up an' join the others,' Wolf Brennan snarled at the fallen Pinkerton man. Matt Lewis scrambled to his feet, clutching his right shoulder. Blood seeped from between his fingers, but he, of all the passengers, looked the least frightened or intimidated. Indeed, he fixed the outlaw chief with a steady, baleful stare.

Meantime, Blue Duck had dismounted and strolled over to where Donnie Quick lay dying. Seeing that the shot-gun guard was not quite dead, the Comanche straightaway aimed his revolver at Quick's head and blasted his brains out.

'OK, boys, go see what's in these folks' luggage,' snapped Brennan. Then, turning to Lo-Lo McCoy and Pawnee Pete, he said, 'You an' me, we'll search their persons.' So saying, he swiftly dismounted, followed by the rest of his gang. While the outlaws, under the direction of Blue Duck, pulled the various portmanteaus, suitcases and baggages down off the roof of the stagecoach and proceeded to rip them open and rifle through their contents, Wolf Brennan and his other two lieutenants conducted a thorough search of the travellers themselves.

Little of any value was found amongst the luggage. However, the search of the passengers' persons proved rather more successful. Both salesmen were stripped of their wallets, which were stuffed full of banknotes. Buddy Jones was also relieved of a fine old gold hunter, while the Reverend Frank Sanders lost a half-hunter and a small wad of ten-dollar bills. Annie Sanders handed over several items of jewellery and Kitty O'Hara reluctantly bade farewell to her derringer and her life's savings. As for Matt Lewis, Lo-Lo McCoy took his wallet and then, from a pocket hidden deep inside the Pinkerton agent's coat, a small, slim rectangular-shaped box. He opened it and gasped.

'Jeez, Wolf! Look what we've got here!' he exclaimed and pulled out a magnificent diamond necklace that fairly sparkled in the sunlight. 'Do you reckon these here stones are the real thing?' he asked excitedly.

'Lemme see,' snapped Brennan.

McCoy stretched out his hand towards his chief and Brennan grabbed hold of the necklace. He was studying it when, suddenly, a shot rang out and Lo-Lo McCoy gasped and keeled over.

Three further shots rang out. One missed its mark, but two did not, and two more of Wolf Brennan's men bit the dust, to lie motionless on the trail, blood oozing from the bullet-wounds in their chests.

This totally unexpected attack immediately threw the outlaws into a panic and they began firing wildly in all directions. Even Wolf Brennan and Blue Duck, the most experienced of the desperadoes, failed to keep their heads. They observed that the shots were coming from behind a cluster of boulders situated in front of them, on Coyote Gulch's eastern ridge. Consequently, anxious not to present their attackers with an easy target, they hastily dived into the cover of a nearby scattering of rocks. But they had omitted to grab hold of their rifles from their saddle-boots and their unseen enemy proved to be beyond the range of their revolvers. Brennan cursed and rammed the diamond necklace into the inside pocket of his black leather jacket.

The rest of the gang, meantime, were also desperately looking for rocks behind which to shelter. Five of the seven succeeded in doing so, while the others fell victim to the murderous fire raining down on them from the ridge. Amongst the fallen was the rotund figure of Pawnee Pete, a neat red patch showing in the middle of his yellow bandanna, where the bullet had penetrated his forehead.

'Goddammit, there ain't but six of us left!' cried Brennan.

Blue Duck grunted.

'We go,' he said tersely.

'Yeah. Those bastards are out of range, though mebbe if'n we take a hostage. . . .' Brennan glanced towards the spot where the travellers had earlier been grouped together. During the course of the shooting, however, they had all scrambled back into the comparative safety of the stagecoach. 'No! That ain't gonna work,' he muttered disconsolately.

'We go,' repeated Blue Duck.

Brennan noted that a few of their horses had already cantered off, while the others trotted nervously back and forth, or in circles, in obvious fright. He cursed himself for having abandoned them in favour of a place of refuge amongst the rocks. And he continued to curse as he recalled slipping his Colt Hartford into his saddle-boot immediately before riding down into Coyote Gulch. Why hadn't he thought to take it with when he dived for cover? By blasting away with their handguns, the outlaws were simply wasting precious ammunition.

'We go,' said Blue Duck for a third time.

'Yeah,' said Brennan. 'But let's do this right. We gotta git outa here darned quick or them sonsofbitches up on that ridge'll shoot us dead sure as hell.'

'It is very bad,' commented Blue Duck.

'Not so bad. Not if we *do* git away,' said Brennan.

'What do you mean?' enquired the Comanche.

'Wa'al, I got this here diamond necklace an' most of the folks' cash. Lo-Lo an' Pawnee Pete was holdin' some of the loot, but if'n we git outa here, we still got plenty to split between us.'

'And fewer to claim a share,' grinned Blue Duck.

'That's right,' replied Brennan.

Of the original dozen under his command, a mere five remained alive. If he counted himself, Brennan mused, there had been thirteen in the gang. Unlucky for some. Dead unlucky.

Wolf Brennan glanced to his left and to his right. His followers were pinned down behind the scattering of rocks and continuing to exchange fire with their unseen and unknown attackers, though with no hope of hitting them. How many of them were there, he wondered?

'Cease firin'!' he yelled. 'They are well outa range.'

'So, whaddya suggest we do?' retorted Red Dawson, the last surviving half-breed. He had a Kiowa brave for a father and a redheaded Irishwoman for a mother. 'We cain't jest sit tight an' do nuthin'.'

'No. We gotta make a run for it. But we do so in an orderly manner,' said Brennan. 'I can see my hoss, but some of the others have vamoosed.'

'Yea, mine's gone,' yelled one of the gang.

'An' so's mine,' cried another.

'An' mine,' added a third.

'Wa'al, jest so there's no confusion, sort out now which of the remainin' hosses you're each gonna grab. Otherwise, it's likely two or more of you will make for the same hoss an' the result'll be chaos.'

It took only a few moments for the outlaws to do as their chief had instructed. Each man having claimed his horse, they immediately indicated their readiness to depart.

'OK. Then let's lam outa here,' snapped Brennan.

The six bandits hurriedly rose to their feet and, crouching as they ran, zig-zagged across the open ground to where the remaining horses neighed and pranced nervously. Quickly, they calmed the skittish animals and mounted them. Their corkscrew run had, to some extent, caused the riflemen on the ridge to miss their aim, though two of the outlaws were hit, one before he could reach his horse and the other as he was heaving himself up into the saddle.

From inside the stagecoach, the victims of the hold-up watched the rout. The Reverend Frank Sanders and his wife both clasped their hands together and offered up prayers of thanksgiving to the Lord, while Buddy Jones and Ned Burns cheered loudly every time one of the outlaws was gunned down. But Matt Lewis neither prayed nor cheered, as he slumped back in his seat, still clutching his wounded shoulder. Not until the one possessing the diamond necklace was shot down, would he feel like smiling, let alone cheering.

Kitty O'Hara, meantime, was urgently considering her situation. Her escape from the forces of law and order had seemed almost certain. But now she was penniless and her chance of getting to Dallas was no longer assured, for there was every likelihood that Billy Tranter's body had been discovered. And, if this was so, then a posse could well be in hot pursuit, since her departure on the stage had not gone unnoticed. Anyway, even should she reach Dallas, what would she do then? Without money, she would be unable to obtain a rail ticket. She would be stuck in Dallas until the posse eventually arrived.

The redhead thought hard. She had to do something fast. But what? Kitty watched the outlaws scramble up from behind the rocks and run towards their horses. Then an idea struck her. It was a wild and desperate measure, but she believed it was the only course left open to her if she was to avoid capture. She would have to throw in her lot with the outlaws.

Therefore, much to the surprise and alarm of her fellow travellers, Kitty suddenly jumped up and leapt out of the stagecoach.

'Where d'you think you're goin'?' cried Buddy Jones.

'Yes. Where indeed?' exclaimed the Reverend Frank Sanders.

But Kitty ignored their cries. She ran as fast as she could towards the nearest of the outlaws. He happened to be their leader, Wolf Brennan. As he clambered into the saddle, she stretched out a hand and grabbed hold of his horse's bridle.

'Hey, mister,' she cried. 'Can I ride with you?'

Brennan stared at the redhead in amazement.

'Leggo that goddam bridle!' he rasped.

Kitty did as she was bid, but stood her ground.

'Please! Please let me ride with you!' she pleaded.

'You crazy?' he snarled. Then, seeing her imploring look, he relented and said, 'OK! OK! Grab yourself a hoss an' follow me.'

Brennan dug his heels into his horse's flanks and set off at a gallop. In the meantime, the other surviving outlaws had mounted their horses, and they were quick to follow their leader. He headed back down the gulch, in the direction from which the stagecoach had come. Consequently, he and his men were soon out of range of their attackers' rifles.

Kitty mounted one of the spare horses, a sorrel, but with some difficulty. Hitching up her skirt and, at the same time, mounting a skittish horse was by no means an easy exercise. Twice the redhead attempted it and twice she failed. However, at the third attempt, she finally succeeded in heaving herself into the saddle. Then, turning the sorrel's head, she sent the beast racing after the fast-departing outlaws.

Her erstwhile companions watched in bewilderment as the redhead disappeared from view round a bend in the trail. They looked at each other in stunned silence. Finally, Buddy Jones spoke.

'Wa'al, I'll be darned!' he exclaimed.

And so it was that the five of them disembarked from the stagecoach, thankful that the bandits had been routed, though mourning their losses and completely nonplussed by Kitty O'Hara's sudden, unexpected desertion.

FOUR

The travellers stood beside the stage and watched as two men appeared on top of the ridge and began to ride slowly down to the floor of Coyote Gulch. One of them rode a bay gelding, while the other was mounted on a piebald mare.

The man riding the gelding was a big, wide-shouldered Kentuckian, six foot two inches tall and weighing approximately two hundred pounds. Cool pale-blue eyes peered out of a rugged, weather-beaten face, the nose of which had been broken sometime in the past, and the brown hair, which showed beneath the brim of the man's Stetson, was liberally speckled with grey. A red kerchief was tied round his neck, and he wore a knee-length buckskin jacket over a grey shirt and well-worn blue denim pants. He carried a Frontier Model Colt in his holster and a Winchester in his saddle-boot.

51

His companion looked to be at least ten years his junior and he, too, wore a Stetson and had a kerchief tied round his neck. Black-haired, with an open, youthful countenance, the younger man was clad in the traditional garb of the cowboy, namely check shirt, brown leather vest, blue Levis beneath a pair of leather chaps, and boots and spurs. Like the big man, he carried a Winchester in his saddleboot, but his choice of handgun was a Remington.

By the time the two men reached the stagecoach, the passengers had recovered some of their possessions from the outlaws' corpses and the Reverend Frank Sanders and his wife had begun tending Matt Lewis's shoulder wound. It was, therefore, Buddy Jones who greeted them.

'Gee, fellers!' he exclaimed. 'I guess we owe you our lives.'

'Oh, come now, Mr Jones, I think it was our valuables, rather than our lives, that those miscreants were intent upon taking,' interjected the clergyman. 'Nevertheless, thank you for your intervention, gentlemen. Allow me to introduce myself. The Reverend Frank Sanders at your service.'

'Good day to you, Reverend,' replied the big man. 'My name's Stone, Jack Stone. An' this here's Phil Marsh.'

'Howdy, folks,' said the younger man.

At this point introductions were made all round

and, once these formalities had been completed, the wounded Pinkerton agent asked curiously, 'How come you chanced to be here? Were you on the trail of them outlaws, Mr Stone?'

'No, Mr Lewis, I wasn't,' replied Stone.

'I only wondered 'cause you're somethin' of a legend in the West. Ain't you the man who tamed Mallory, the roughest, toughest town in Colorado?' enquired Lewis.

'I am,' confirmed Stone. 'But, on this occasion, I was pursuin' nobody. Nope; me an' Phil, we was simply headin' south to San Antonio, where we intend signin' on for the annual cattle drive up the Goodnight-Loving trail to Cheyenne.'

'That's right,' said Phil Marsh. 'Mr Stone an' I met up jest outside Fort Smith, an' we've been ridin' south together ever since. 'Course, I got another reason to head for San Antonio. Y'see, it's my home town.'

'Ah, so you're a Texan!' said Annie Sanders.

'Born an' bred.'

'We were about to enter the northern end of this here gulch when we heard shots,' explained Stone, adding, 'Instead, we rode up on to the ridge, where we had a bird's eye view of the hold-up.'

'It was real easy pickin' off them thievin' varmints from up there,' added Phil Marsh gleefully.

'Unfortunately, some of 'em got clean away,' growled Stone.

'With a lot of our money,' sighed Ned Burns.

'That's right,' agreed Buddy Jones.

'More'n jest money,' said Matt Lewis.

The Pinkerton man had, by now, had his wound bandaged and his arm put into a sling. Both the bandages and the sling were composed of strips torn from one of the Reverend Sanders's spare shirts. Annie tossed the remaining shreds of the shirt into the portmanteau from which she had extracted it.

'Yes,' she said. 'The bandit chief, the one dressed all in black, also made off with a diamond necklace. Yours, I believe?'

'No,' said Lewis. 'It didn't belong to me. It was the property of a Mrs Elspeth Worthing, a rich widow who died a few days back in the town of Sweetwater.'

'Oh!'

'She had left it in her will to a niece livin' in Dallas. Her lawyers contacted the Pinkerton Detective Agency an' arranged for one of its agents to transport the necklace from their offices in Sweetwater to the niece's home in Dallas. I was the agent chosen to carry out this task.'

'An' you've blown it,' commented Stone.

'Yeah.' Lewis frowned. 'I sure ain't lookin' forward to explainin' what's happened to Mr Pinkerton.'

Stone nodded. Allan Pinkerton, who had created the agency a few years earlier in Chicago, was a hard-headed Scot, not noted for his tolerance of failure.

He expected his agents to succeed in whatever task or investigation he assigned to them. The loss of the diamond necklace would not only damage the Pinkerton Agency's reputation, it would cost them a great deal of money. Matt Lewis's despondency was, therefore, quite understandable.

'Wa'al, mebbe the law will catch up with them outlaws an' then—' began the Kentuckian.

'But who were they?' demanded Lewis, cutting Stone short.

'We got a pretty darned good look at 'em,' said Ned Burns.

'That's right,' concurred the Reverend Sanders. 'Once we arrive at our next port of call – where is that, by the way?'

'Cactus City,' said Stone.

'Wa'al, once there, we must head for the law office and take a look through the Wanted posters. I'm sure we shall be able to identify some of the men who held us up.'

'But they were all masked,' said Annie.

'Even so,' said the clergyman, 'most of their masks slipped down during the gunfight.'

'Their leader, the man in black, had a livid white scar on his face,' added Buddy Jones.

'Yeah, I figure that sonofabitch is the notorious desperado who's been terrorizin' folks in these parts for some li'l time. He's famous for always wearin' nuthin' but black,' said Ned Burns.

The others all turned and stared at the whiskey salesman.

'So, who d' you reckon he is?' asked Lewis.

'A no-account critter named Wolf Brennan. One of my customers was tellin' me 'bout him jest the other day,' said Burns.

'Wolf Brennan, eh? I s'pose the Agency could put a price on his head,' said Lewis, adding glumly, ' 'Course, that won't help me none.'

'Nope, an' you sure ain't in no shape to go after him an' his gang,' ventured Stone.

'Mr Stone's right,' said Annie. 'We've bandaged you up an' staunched the flow of blood, but you need to get a doctor to extract the bullet.'

'I realize that,' said the Pinkerton agent. 'Also, I'll needs telegraph my Chicago office jest as soon as we arrive in Cactus City.'

'But the driver's dead. So, who's going to drive the stagecoach?' enquired Annie. She turned to her husband. 'Frank, you can handle a gig. Could you manage that team of horses?'

The clergyman shook his head.

'I don't think so, my dear, though I could try,' he replied doubtfully.

'Wa'al, don't look at me. I cain't even ride a hoss,' declared Buddy Jones.

'Me neither,' said Ned Burns.

'If it weren't for this wound, I guess I could probably handle them hosses,' said Lewis.

'I'll do it,' growled Stone.

'But you said you were heading for San Antonio. That's in quite the opposite direction,' remarked the Reverend Sanders.

'Cactus City ain't much above an hour away. It's a diversion I can easily make,' declared the Kentuckian.

'Gee, Jack, what about that thar cattle drive?' asked Phil Marsh anxiously. 'If'n we don't git to San Antonio in time—'

'We should git there with a few days to spare, Phil.'

'But—'

Stone smiled.

'I know. You wanta look up some of your kin 'fore the cattle drive begins.'

'I ain't been home in two years,' confessed the young Texan. 'Guess I was hopin' to spend some time with my folks while I waited for the drive to start.'

'Then go ahead.'

'Whaddya mean?'

'You ride on. I'll drive the stage to Cactus City. If I make it down to San Antonio in time to join the cattle drive, I'll be seein' you. If not, then it's so long, pardner.'

Phil Marsh looked undecided.

'You sure, Jack?' he asked.

'Yup.' The Kentuckian stretched out his hand. 'Have yourself a safe ride,' he said.

'Thanks. I'll miss your company.'

The two men shook hands and then the Texan mounted his piebald mare. He turned her head towards the south.

'*Adios, amigo!*' he cried and promptly set off through Coyote Gulch in the direction taken earlier by Wolf Brennan and his diminished band of outlaws.

'OK, folks,' said Stone, once his erstwhile companion had disappeared from sight, 'if'n you'll board the stage, I'll see about drivin' you all to Cactus City.'

While the clergyman and his wife and the two salesmen clambered into the coach, the Kentuckian set about securing his horse to its rear with a length of whipcord, which he attached to the animal's bridle. It was his intention that the gelding should trot along quite happily in the wake of the stagecoach. He patted the animal reassuringly and then turned and headed towards the box, where he found Matt Lewis awaiting him.

'Ain't you gittin' on board?' he demanded.

'I figure I'll ride up on the box with you,' replied Lewis. 'If that's OK?'

The Kentuckian shrugged his broad shoulders.

'That's fine by me, though it might be more comfortable for you inside,' he said, eyeing the Pinkerton man's wounded shoulder.

'I'd prefer to ride on the box,' stated Lewis firmly.

'OK.'

Stone helped the Pinkerton agent climb up and quickly followed him. Then he grabbed the reins and set the stagecoach in motion. As it proceeded on its journey through Coyote Gulch, it began to pick up speed.

Inside the stage, the four passengers were frankly relieved to be continuing on their journey. They conversed excitedly, recalling the hold-up, and talking of the various items and amounts of money taken. Then the Reverend Sanders mentioned the defection of Kitty O'Hara. They all looked at the empty seat where the redhead had been sitting, and began to discuss her unexpected and unexplained departure. On the box, Jack Stone brought up the same subject.

'That young woman who left the stage an' rode off with Wolf Brennan an' his gang. What did you make of that?' he asked.

'I dunno,' said a mystified Matt Lewis.

'Who was she?'

'Wa'al, she called herself Kitty O'Hara. Said she was goin' to Dallas to visit her sister. Like Mrs Sanders. Only Mrs Sanders's sister is sick. I dunno 'bout Miss O'Hara's.'

'Mebbe there is no such sister?'

'Mebbe.'

'D'you think she was in cahoots with the outlaws?'

'I dunno what to think, Mr Stone. I mean, she played no active part in the hold-up. An' I would've sworn that she was jest as surprised an' scared as the rest of us when the stage was held up.' Lewis scratched his head and continued, 'Also, one of the outlaws took her reticule an' emptied it. Why would he have done that if Miss O'Hara was in cahoots with them?'

The Kentuckian frowned and shook his head.

'Beats me,' he said.

'Yet she rode off of her own free will,' admitted the young Pinkerton man.

'Sure looked that way to me.'

'It's a goddam mystery.'

'Yup,' said Stone, as he flicked the reins and sent the stagecoach rattling out of the mouth of Coyote Gulch and on to the plain beyond.

FIVE

Johnnie Tranter rode hell-for-leather along the trail, hoping to overtake the stagecoach before it reached its next staging-post, Cactus City. But, despite the delay occasioned by the hold-up, he was unable to do so, for Jack Stone had maintained a rare pace since taking over the reins. Anxious to discharge his responsibility and then resume his journey, the Kentuckian had not spared the horses. They were, in consequence, well-nigh exhausted when the stage eventually drew up in front of Cactus City's stage-line depot at a few minutes past six o' clock that evening. Johnnie Tranter, on the other hand, did not succeed in reaching Cactus City until dusk was falling, a good half-hour after the arrival of the stagecoach.

He pulled up his black stallion outside the Golden Spur Saloon and dismounted. Then, having hitched his mount to the rail in front of the saloon, he entered through its batwing doors.

The bar-room was like a hundred others across the length and breadth of the West. Brass lamps hung from rough wooden rafters; there was a scattering of tables and chairs; games of chance, including poker, blackjack, faro and roulette, were in progress; at one end stood a small, curtained stage and at the other the bar, with its marbled top and large rectangular mirror. There were two pot-bellied stoves, both unlit, and several spittoons, and the bar-room floor was lightly sprinkled with sawdust.

Johnnie Tranter elbowed his way through the crowd surrounding the bar and ordered a beer. Although anxious to pick up Kitty O'Hara, he reckoned that he could afford to leave her a while longer in the custody of the town marshal, where he naturally assumed her to be. His wild ride had given him one heck of a thirst and he determined to assuage it before heading for the law office.

As he stood, quietly savouring his drink, he chanced to overhear the conversation of the two men standing next to him. One was the *Cactus City Chronicle*'s chief reporter, a lanky, loose-limbed fellow named Luke Shaw, and the other a local homesteader, Ben Brogan.

'You heard 'bout the stage, Ben?' enquired the lanky reporter.

'No. I jest rode into town a coupla minutes back,'

replied the homesteader.

' 'Course you did! Wa'al, the stage got held up out at Coyote Gulch,' said Luke Shaw.

'It did?'

'Yeah, by that murderin', no-account sonofabitch Wolf Brennan an' his gang.'

'I hear tell he'd recently recruited some new members. Got hisself a pretty big outfit.'

'Not any more. Seems there was one helluva gunfight an' he lost several of his men.'

'But did he escape?'

'Yeah. Him an' the rest of 'em took off. God knows where they are by now.'

Tranter was tempted to butt in and put a few questions, which he had in mind to ask. However, he wasn't sure quite how much the lanky man knew. Therefore, instead, he quickly downed his beer and left the saloon. The young man had spied the law office on his way into town. He hurriedly directed his steps towards it.

He found the marshal alone in the office, his deputies being out, doing their rounds of the town.

Marshal Luther Grey was a large, florid-faced man in his late forties. He was sitting behind his desk, smoking a cheroot and idly flicking through a pile of 'Wanted' notices. He glanced up as the Texan threw open the office door and strode purposefully across the room and up to the desk.

'Can I help you, Mr, er—?' began the lawman.

'Captain,' said Tranter. 'Captain John Tranter of the Texas Rangers.'

'Ah, yes!' Marshal Luther Grey frowned. 'I received a wire from Sheriff Dunn in Double Drop, informin' me that you—'

'The stage, I'm told it was held up,' Johnnie Tranter interrupted him.

'That's so.' Luther Grey scowled darkly. 'A bad business,' he said. 'Both the driver an' the guard were shot dead.'

'An' the stage? I passed through Coyote Gulch, but I didn't see it.'

'No. It was like this. Two fellers, headin' south, chanced to spot the hold-up from the ridge above Coyote Gulch. They opened fire on the outlaws, killin' seven of 'em an' sendin' the others packin'.'

'Holy cow!'

'Yeah. Afterwards, one of the two fellers continued on his journey, while the other stayed an' drove the stage the rest of the way here, to Cactus City.'

'Did he indeed?'

'Yup. His name is Jack Stone. He's been many things in his time: Army scout, depitty US Marshal, sheriff. Hell, the man is a livin' legend!'

Johnnie Tranter nodded.

'Yeah, I've heard of him. It was darned lucky he an' his pal turned up when they did.'

'Sure was.'

'So, what about the passengers? Did they all survive?'

'Er, yeah, they did. But you ain't gonna like this,' muttered the marshal, his shrewd blue eyes gazing anxiously at the Texas Ranger.

'What ain't I gonna like?' snapped Tranter.

'There were six of 'em altogether.' Luther Grey paused and picked up a single sheet of paper, which had been lying next to his pile of Wanted notices. He peered at it and read as follows: 'The Reverend Frank and Mrs Sanders, Mr Buddy Jones, Mr Ned Burns, Mr Matt Lewis an' Miss Kitty O'Hara.' He emphasized the last-named and then added, 'Mr Lewis suffered a shoulder wound, but the rest were unhurt.'

'An' are they all here in Cactus City?'

'Not all of 'em, no. Five are, an' they're hopin' to resume their journey to Dallas tomorrow mornin'. The stage-line are providin' a fresh driver an' guard.'

A sudden premonition struck Johnnie Tranter. The marshal had said he wasn't going to like something. It could only be. . . .

'The sixth passenger, the one who ain't here in Cactus City; let me guess which,' he said.

'Go ahead, Cap'n.'

'Would it be Miss Kitty O'Hara?'

'It would.'

'So, what happened to Miss O'Hara?'

'You ain't gonna believe this.'

'Try me.'

'She lit out with the outlaws.'

'She did what?' exclaimed the Texas Ranger incredulously.

'I said you wouldn't believe it.'

'Was she in cahoots with the outlaws, d'you think?' enquired Tranter, echoing the question, which Jack Stone had put earlier to the Pinkerton agent, Matt Lewis.

'I dunno,' replied the marshal. 'Seems unlikely.'

'Why d'you say that?'

'Wa'al, accordin' to Mr Lewis, she was robbed jest the same as the other passengers.'

'That so?'

'It is. He said one of the outlaws grabbed hold of her reticule an' emptied it. Apparently, he took from it a derringer an' a small wad of banknotes.'

The derringer that killed my kid brother, thought Johnnie Tranter angrily. Aloud, he said, 'Miss Kitty O'Hara is wanted for murder. I was expectin' to pick her up here.'

'I know. Sheriff Dunn's wire said as much.'

'But it seems she's given me the slip.'

'Seems so, Cap'n. She's thrown in her lot with Wolf Brennan an' his associates.'

'Yup.' Tranter stared the lawman straight in the

eye and demanded, 'So, Marshal, what are you doin' 'bout apprehendin' them outlaws?'

'I've telegraphed the sheriffs in this an' the neighbourin' counties, advisin' 'em to keep a look-out for the gang.'

'You didn't think to round up a posse an'—?'

'No point, Cap'n. It's already dusk outside. How're we s'posed to find 'em in the dark? Anyways, they'll be long gone by now. Hell, when they fled Coyote Gulch, they could've headed north, south, east or west!' Luther Grey sighed and added wearily, 'Personally, I don't hold out much hope that Wolf Brennan an' his gang will be caught. That's one helluva big country we gotta search. 'Course, one of the county sheriffs might git lucky.'

And pigs might fly, mused Tranter. He smiled sourly.

'OK,' he said. 'Guess you've done all you can.'

'You still proposin' to pursue your fugitive?' enquired the marshal.

'I am. I don't give up easy,' replied Tranter.

'So, what's your next move?'

'I'm not sure. Mebbe I'll have me a few words with Miss O'Hara's fellow passengers? D' you know where I can find 'em?'

'We got two hotels in town. Most of 'em booked into the Alhambra, but Mr Lewis an' Mr Stone, they're stayin' at Flinder's Hotel.'

'Hmm. Reckon I'll make a start at Flinder's Hotel then. Where is it located?'

'Almost directly across the street.'

'That's handy, Marshal. Thanks for your time.'

'A pleasure, Cap'n, an' I sure hope you do succeed in catchin' up with Miss O'Hara.'

'You can depend on it,' declared the young Texas Ranger confidently.

Thereupon, he turned on his heel and swiftly left the law office.

A few minutes later, he found Matt Lewis and Jack Stone dining together in the hotel's restaurant.

Although the Kentuckian had intended to turn round and head south just as soon as he had driven the stagecoach into Cactus City and explained matters to the town marshal, things had not exactly turned out that way. Lewis had insisted upon buying him a drink before he set off and, as the ride had given him a considerable thirst, Stone had gratefully accepted the other's offer.

Then, before Stone could say that he needed to be off, Lewis had clutched him by the arm and said, 'Look, I shall have to git this darned wound properly attended to, but, before I go see the local doctor, I wanta ask you a favour.'

'Oh, yeah. What kinda favour?' enquired Stone warily.

'I was entrusted by the Pinkerton Agency to

transport a diamond necklace from Sweetwater to Dallas.'

'So you said earlier. The property of some deceased widow woman, which was intended for her niece.'

'The beneficiary. That's right.' Lewis grimaced. 'I'm gonna have to report its loss to Mr Pinkerton,' he groaned.

'You mentioned you weren't lookin' forward to that.'

'I ain't, Mr Stone.'

'So, what can I do to help? I don't see—'

'I want you to go after Wolf Brennan an' retrieve that necklace.'

'Hell, no!'

'In my opinion, the chances of his gittin' caught by any of the local sheriffs are pretty remote. But, if'n you rode out to Coyote Gulch, you could mebbe pick up the sonofabitch's trail. I heard you were 'bout as good a tracker as any Kiowa brave.'

'No white man's that good.'

'But you could pick up his tracks?'

'I guess.'

'So, will you do it, Mr Stone? I mean, I cain't go after Brennan, not with this goddam shoulder injury.'

'No, that's for sure.'

'Wa'al?'

'I told you, I'm aimin' to head south an' join a cattle drive.'

'I figure the Agency can match any wages you're likely to git on that cattle drive.' Lewis smiled wryly and explained, 'When I wire Mr Pinkerton, informin' him 'bout the diamond necklace, I wanta tell him that all is not lost, that you have agreed to try to retrieve it. I'm certain he'll be only too happy to recruit you an' pay you the usual wage, with the promise of a hefty bonus should you succeed in recoverin' it. So, whaddya say?'

'Hmm. I dunno.'

'I don't expect you to tackle Wolf Brennan an' his gang all on your lonesome. Jest track 'em to their hide-out, then head on into the nearest town an' contact the local peace officer.'

'An' lead that peace officer an' his posse out to Brennan's lair?'

'That's right.'

'Wa'al, mebbe. . . .' Stone paused and took a deep draught of beer.

He pondered the situation, reflecting that he had fairly recently teamed up with another Pinkerton man and, together, they had succeeded in bringing to book the notorious outlaw, Scotch John MacGregor. This time, however, he would not exactly be teaming up with Matt Lewis; he would be going it alone.

'You surely ain't gonna let that murderin', no-

70

account varmint git clean away?' demanded Lewis.

Stone sighed deeply.

'I s'pose not,' he muttered. 'OK. You've convinced me.'

And so the matter had been settled. The Kentuckian had stayed, proposing to set out for Coyote Gulch at first light.

Now they were approached by Johnnie Tranter, who, upon entering the restaurant, had quickly looked round and observed the two men sitting together, one of whom had his right shoulder bandaged and his arm in a sling. He had immediately guessed that they were the ones he was seeking.

'Name's Tranter,' he said, 'Captain John Tranter of the Texas Rangers. I believe you gentlemen are Mr Jack Stone an' Mr Matt Lewis?'

'Yup. I'm Stone an' my friend's Mr Lewis. How can we help you, Cap'n?' growled the Kentuckian.

'It's 'bout that hold-up in Coyote Gulch,' said Tranter.

'Oh, yeah?'

'Yeah. Y'see, one of the passengers in the stagecoach is a fugitive from justice, a fugitive whom I'm pursuin'.'

'Miss Kitty O'Hara?' said Lewis.

'Right. A good guess.'

'It wasn't a guess. Had your fugitive been one of the other passengers, you'd have gone straight to the

Alhambra rather than here.'

'I'm informed that Miss O'Hara lit out with the outlaws who attacked the stage.'

'Correct.'

'I'm also informed that she went voluntarily.'

'Yup.'

'But we don't believe she was in cahoots with Brennan an' his gang,' said Stone.

'No?'

'No, for she was robbed same as the other passengers.'

'An' what did the outlaws steal from you, Mr Lewis?' enquired the Texas Ranger.

'A diamond necklace, which was in my keeping,' replied Lewis.

'Wow!'

'Yeah. Mr Stone has agreed to help me retrieve it.'

'You're goin' after Wolf Brennan?'

'I'm not.' Lewis indicated his bandaged shoulder. After Jack Stone had agreed to pursue the outlaws, Lewis had called upon the town's doctor, who had removed the bullet and dressed the wound again. 'The Agency has engaged Mr Stone's services,' he explained.

'The Agency?'

'I'm a Pinkerton man. The necklace belongs to a client. I wired Chicago an' it's all settled. Mr Stone is gonna try to track down the Brennan gang while I continue on to Dallas. If Mr Stone succeeds in findin' their hide-out, he'll report its whereabouts to the nearest available peace officer.'

'I see.'

Johnnie Tranter gave the matter some thought. Had Kitty O'Hara not ridden off with the outlaws, he would surely have caught up with her either at the Alhambra or at Flinder's Hotel. Now, if he wanted to apprehend his brother's killer, he needs must track down Wolf Brennan and his associates. He eyed the Kentuckian speculatively.

'You got somethin' on your mind?' growled Stone.

'As a matter of fact, I have,' said Tranter.

'Wa'al, spit it out.'

'I was wonderin', Mr Stone, whether mebbe you could do with some company when you set out after the Brennan gang?'

'You aimin' to join me, then?'

'I'd sure like to. If 'n when you find Wolf Brennan, you're also gonna find Miss Kitty O'Hara.'

'Your fugitive, Cap'n,'

'That's right.'

'What's she s'posed to have done?' enquired Matt Lewis, intrigued.

'Shot a man dead.' Tranter smiled thinly. 'The sheriff back in Double Drop has charged me with bringin' her in to face trial.'

' 'Deed? An' jest who was this feller she shot?'

'A decent, upright citizen, a young man who—'

'So, how an' why'd she shoot him?'

Tranter fixed the Pinkerton agent with a stony stare, before answering coldly, 'She lured him up to her room an' then, havin' shot him, took all his money.'

'Then robbery was the motive for the murder?' said Lewis.

'It was,' lied Tranter, whereupon he turned to face the big Kentuckian. 'Wa'al, Mr Stone, whaddya say? Can I ride with you?' he asked anxiously.

Stone carefully considered the other's proposition. That the sheriff back in Double Drop should have engaged the services of the Texas Ranger to hunt down Kitty O'Hara made sense. Yet his instincts told him that there was something not quite right about this arrangement. And Stone's instincts rarely let him down. Nevertheless, he could think of no reason to refuse Tranter's request.

'OK, Cap'n,' he drawled. 'You can ride with me, providin' you follow my orders.' Johnnie Tranter frowned. As a captain in the Texas Rangers, he was more used to giving, than taking, orders.

'An' jest what are your orders?' he enquired.

'If we do succeed in trackin' the Brennan gang to their hide-out, you don't go ridin' in there with guns blazin'. You an' me, we quietly ride off an' fetch help. Then we return to Wolf Brennan's hide-out with a good-sized posse.' Stone paused to let his words sink in, before continuing, 'That way, we're likely to catch

74

all of 'em.'

Tranter had to concede that the Kentuckian had a point. Should the two of them attempt to tackle the outlaws on their own, there was every chance that some of the miscreants, including his quarry, might escape.

'OK,' he said. 'We do it your way.'

'Fine!'

'I guess you'll be aimin' to set out for Coyote Gulch as soon as it's light?'

'That's right.'

'Wa'al, let me buy you fellers a drink,' said Tranter. 'I figure a toast is called for.'

Jack Stone and the Pinkerton man had by now finished their meal. Therefore, they adjourned to the bar-room, where Johnnie Tranter ordered and paid for three beers. He turned to the others and raised his glass.

'To the capture of both the Brennan gang an' Miss Kitty O'Hara!' he cried.

The three men swiftly downed large draughts of the amber liquid.

'This is gonna be my last tonight,' declared Stone. 'Tomorrow, I'll sure as hell need all my wits about me.'

'Me, too,' said Tranter.

Matt Lewis nodded gravely. If he was to have any chance of retrieving the Widow Worthing's diamond necklace, he needed Jack Stone and the Texas Ranger to be at their very best.

SIX

Wolf Brennan galloped across the plain, pursued by his depleted band of outlaws and Kitty O'Hara.

Of the original gang, only one renegade Comanche remained – Blue Duck – while the sole surviving half-breed was the red-headed, and aptly named, Red Dawson. The white men in Wolf Brennan's gang had fared rather better. Excluding Brennan himself, three others had escaped Jack Stone's and Phil Marsh's deadly fire. They were two Irish-American brothers, Pat and Danny Doyle, squat, mean-eyed, heavily bearded ruffians, and Fred Carter, a tall, lugubrious-looking fellow in a long, ankle-length brown leather coat and a tall, badly dented stovepipe hat.

They headed towards the hill country surrounding the Trinity river. Their intended destination was a deserted ranch house in one of several valleys leading off from the river. The Double B ranch, once owned by a cousin of Wolf Brennan, had long since failed. However, the ranch house would provide a reasonably comfortable and secluded retreat, where the gang could hide out and ponder on their next move.

The light was beginning to fade when this motley band eventually entered the valley and approached the ranch house. Much to their relief, it remained in a moderately good state of repair. Weary, dusty and saddle-sore, they thankfully dismounted and hitched their horses to the rail in front of the house.

Wolf Brennan led the way up the short flight of wooden steps to the stoop. He clumped across it and pushed open the ranch house door. Inside was a large rectangular-shaped chamber, which had evidently once been the rancher's living-room, dining-room and kitchen combined. Behind a couple of doors at its far end were two bedrooms. All three rooms were completely devoid of furniture.

'Gee, there ain't nuthin' here!' groaned Fred Carter.

'Whaddya expect?' snarled Wolf Brennan. 'The place has been empty for a coupla years or more.'

'We cain't stay here. Without food an' water—'

'I ain't plannin' to stay long, Fred,' retorted Brennan.

'How long?'

'Jest overnight. There's a well out back an' a small paddock, where we can graze our hosses. We're all carryin' beef jerky an' hard tack, so we ain't gonna starve.'

'Guess not.'

'We decide on our next move an' then set out at first light. That's the plan,' said Brennan. 'For now, we see to the hosses an' then bring our saddles an' saddle-bags inside. We can hunker down here for the night. It'll be a mite warmer than outside beneath the stars.'

'Yes, we do that,' said Blue Duck decisively, and he turned and quickly stepped outside.

The others followed the Comanche and set about watering their horses and hobbling them in the small paddock behind the ranch house. Then they filled their water-flasks and brought them and the rest of their equipment into the house.

Upon Kitty declaring that she had no flask, Brennan informed her that she could share his. Thereupon, they settled down to slake their thirsts and satisfy their hunger with the beef jerky and hard tack. As Red Dawson held the largest supply of these foods, it was he who shared them with Kitty.

While they were eating, he eyed Kitty curiously and asked, 'Why'd you hightail it with us?'

'Yeah, I've been wonderin' 'bout that,' confessed Brennan.

'I guess we all have,' said Pat Doyle.

'Sure have,' agreed his brother.

Blue Duck and Fred Carter said nothing, though they were as intrigued as the others regarding the redhead's sudden decision to join them in their flight from Coyote Gulch.

'Wa'al, y'see,' said Kitty, 'I didn't fancy endin' my days danglin' at the end of a rope.'

'But why in tarnation would you?' rasped Brennan.

' 'Cause I killed a man.'

'What man?'

'A stinkin', no-account skunk name of Billy Tranter.' Kitty smiled sourly and murmured, 'Let me explain.'

'You do that,' said Brennan.

'My name's Kitty O'Hara an' I'm what you might call a sportin' woman.'

'A whore,' said Fred Carter flatly.

'If you like.' Kitty glared at the outlaw, then turned to face Brennan and continued, 'I was workin' at the Longhorn Saloon in Double Drop. Billy Tranter wanted pleasurin', but he didn't wanta pay. He drew a knife an' was gonna cut me up, so I shot him.'

Wolf Brennan produced the girl's derringer and showed it to her.

'With this?' he asked.

'Yup.'

'You're claimin' it was self-defence. Right?'

'I am.'

'So, why didn't you remain in Double Drop, if 'n you were innocent of murder?'

' 'Cause Billy Tranter's pa is one of the wealthiest an' most influential men around those parts. I couldn't be sure he wouldn't either bribe or scare the jury into findin' me guilty. It was a chance I jest wasn't prepared to take. When you an' your gang held up the stagecoach, I was headin' for Dallas, where I intended to catch a train bound for Kansas City.'

'Guess our intervention made things kinda awkward for you?'

'Sure did. I reckoned I was almost certain to be pursued, but I had hoped to be safely aboard that train 'fore my pursuers could catch up with me. The hold-up made that very unlikely.'

'So, you lit out with us.' Wolf Brennan smiled at the redhead and said quietly, 'I'm glad you did, Miss O'Hara, for I wouldn't like to think of you bein' strung up by your pretty li'l neck. I'm Wolf Brennan, by the way, the leader of this here outfit.'

'Pleased to meet you, Mr Brennan,' purred the redhead, noting the lecherous look in the outlaw chief's eye and being anxious to keep him sweet. It had occurred to her that her present situation was, to say the least, tricky. She was the only woman in a cabin full of dangerous and, in all probability, lustful desperadoes, and she had no wish to satisfy the carnal desires of all six of them. Rather, she hoped that Brennan would keep her to himself. 'But *do* call me Kitty,' she added, with a provocative twinkle in her bright green eyes.

Before Brennan could respond, Fred Carter cut in.

'OK, so that's Kitty's story. Now let's git down to what really matters,' he snapped.

'Oh, yeah? An' what's that, Fred?' rasped Brennan.

'Our present situation an' where we go from here.'

'Fred's right. We got some talkin' to do,' muttered Red Dawson.

The Doyle brothers nodded their agreement, while Blue Duck remained, as usual, impassive.

'I must admit our first foray as a gang wasn't entirely successful,' conceded Brennan.

'You're darned tootin' it wasn't!' cried Carter. 'Goddammit, we lost more'n half our comp'ny!'

'Yeah. The big idea had been for our three separate gangs to join together under your leadership, Wolf, so as to operate more efficiently,' said Dawson. 'That sure didn't work.'

'Mebbe if'n we'd tackled a bank instead of a stage, like Lo-Lo suggested—' began Danny Doyle.

'Huh!' grunted Carter.

'You blamin' me for our losses, Fred?' enquired Wolf Brennan, a hint of menace in his voice.

The tall, lugubrious-looking outlaw gulped and stared at the floor. He *did* blame Brennan, but he had no intention of actually saying so, for Wolf Brennan was not a man he wished to cross.

'Er . . . no . . . no. 'Course not, Wolf,' he mumbled.

'It was jest darned bad luck,' declared Brennan.

'Yeah. Nobody could've expected them fellers to suddenly appear on that ridge an' start shootin' at us,' remarked Red Dawson.

'Though mebbe . . . mebbe we should've posted somebody up on the ridge, as . . . as a kinda look-out,' said Pat Doyle hesistantly.

Brennan glared at the Irish-American.

'You wanta take over the leadership of this here gang?' he demanded.

'Nope.'

'Then, what *are* you sayin'?'

'I'm sayin' that mebbe we should split up.'

'Split up?'

'Yup. Divide the loot an' go our separate ways.'

'But we've only jest formed! That hold-up was our first venture together,' said Brennan.

'So it was.'

'An' you wanta make it our last?'

'I do,' said Pat Doyle.

'Me, too,' said his brother.

Brennan glanced at the other three members of his gang. Their glum faces did nothing to reassure him.

'What about you fellers?' he growled.

'I'm with Pat,' said Red Dawson.

'Yeah. After all, every peace officer hereabouts is gonna be on the look-out for us. It makes sense to split up an' lie low for a while. Me, I reckon I'll head north for Wyoming an' Providence Flats,' remarked Fred Carter.

'I might ride with you,' said Dawson, for Providence Flats was one of several townships dotted across the West where the law dared not venture. It was a place where desperate men, with a price on their heads, could hide out, safe from the fear of capture. There they could rest until the hue and cry died down and they were ready to set forth on some other nefarious enterprise.

Wolf Brennan scowled and turned to the two Doyle brothers.

'Is Providence Flats where you're aimin' for?' he rasped.

'Nope,' said Pat Doyle. 'That's one helluva ride. I reckon me an' Danny will slip across the border into Mexico.'

'Yeah,' said Danny Doyle. 'We can probably link up with Fernando Lopez an' his outfit. We rode with him a coupla years back.'

Brennan nodded. Lopez was as notorious a bandit on the Mexican side of the border as he was on the Texas side.

'OK,' he growled. 'You prefer to ride with a greaser, guess that's up to you.' He glanced across at the remaining member of his gang. 'What about you, Blue Duck?' he enquired of the Comanche.

'I go back to my people,' said the Indian.

'I see.'

'So, how about dividin' up the loot, Wolf?' said Fred Carter. 'The light's fadin' fast. We'd best do it while we can still see.'

'We could leave that till tomorrow mornin',' suggested the outlaw chief.

His followers smiled grimly and shook their heads.

'No deal,' said Carter. 'We do it now.'

'Then each of us can head out tomorrow as an' when he pleases,' stated Red Dawson.

'That makes sense,' declared Pat Doyle.

And so it was settled. The banknotes were produced and counted and, at Wolf Brennan's command, divided equally between his five associates.

'Now, let's see what else we've got,' he rasped.

The others stood in a circle and watched keenly as he laid out Buddy Jones's gold hunter, the Reverend Frank Sanders's half-hunter, Annie Sanders's items of jewellery and Kitty O'Hara's derringer on the floor in front of them.

'How are we gonna divide that lot between us?' enquired Red Dawson anxiously.

'You ain't,' stated Brennan. 'I am.'

The gang leader handed the gold hunter to Fred Carter and the half-hunter and Kitty's derringer to Red Dawson. Then he divided up Mrs Sanders's jewellery, passing a brooch and two gold ear-rings to Blue Duck and a small pocket-watch and a pearl necklace to the Doyle brothers.

'But you ain't taken nuthin', Wolf!' exclaimed Red Dawson, as he pocketed the half-hunter and the short-barrelled pistol.

'Oh, yes, he has!' cried Fred Carter. 'What about that diamond necklace, which Lo-Lo handed to Wolf jest 'fore he was shot?'

'Yeah. I'd forgotten that,' said Red Dawson. 'You figurin' on keepin' that to yourself, Wolf?' he demanded.

'I surely am,' replied Brennan coolly.

'But, hell, that's probably worth more'n the banknotes an' all them other items put together!' exclaimed Pat Doyle.

'So? I'm still boss of this outfit. Leastways, till we split up. An' I reckon I'm entitled to the lion's share.'

'But—' began Carter.

'You gonna try to take it off me, Fred?' enquired

Brennan, his eyes cold as ice and his voice loaded with menace.

'Wa'al, no. I . . . er—'

'Any of you care to try?'

The five outlaws glanced uneasily at each other. No individual was brave enough to stand up against their chief, for they knew that none of them could hope to out-draw Wolf Brennan.

'You may be darned quick with the gun, Wolf, but you cain't out-shoot all of us,' remarked Carter after a long pause.

Wolf Brennan laughed harshly.

'Mebbe not. But I reckon I can take down two or possibly three of you.' Brennan eyed Fred Carter coldly and asked, 'You willin' to chance that you ain't one of those three, Fred?'

Carter blanched, while his companions looked uncertain about what to say or do next. It was at this crucial juncture that Kitty O'Hara decided to intervene.

'Whaddya propose?' she asked. 'Removin' the diamonds from the necklace an' splittin' 'em between you?'

'That's about it,' said Carter, while the others nodded and grunted their approval.

'As it is, the necklace is certainly worth a great deal of money. But the individual stones ain't gonna be worth very much. I mean, how many would each of you git? An' who's gonna buy 'em off trash like you?

Whoever you try to sell 'em to will realize straightaway that they're stolen goods. No reputable jeweller will touch 'em,' Kitty told them.

'Kitty's right, boys,' said Wolf Brennan.

'Then, why are you so keen to hold on to the necklace?' demanded Pat Doyle.

' 'Cause I got me a fence in Laredo, who will give me a fair price.' Brennan smiled and said quietly, 'Come on, boys, I ain't takin' nuthin' else. Be satisfied with your share of the rest of the loot.'

Blue Duck, his face as impassive as ever, regarded the outlaw chief with his black, fathomless eyes.

'We do as Wolf says. The woman is right. Why risk our lives for a few diamonds that we cannot sell?' he asked.

'I dunno. Mebbe we—' began Carter.

'No, Fred. Let Wolf have his lion's share,' said Red Dawson.

Carter frowned, then, after some thought, slowly nodded his head. He knew nobody who would be prepared to fence his share of the precious stones. Besides, he had a nasty feeling that, in any shoot-out between Wolf Brennan and his confederates, he, Carter, would be Brennan's first target.

'What do you fellers say?' asked the outlaw chief of the Doyle brothers.

'I reckon we'll make do with what we've got,' said Pat Doyle.

'That's right, bro',' agreed Danny.

'Then, let's drink to it,' said Wolf Brennan. 'But outside on the stoop, for it's gittin' kinda dark in here.'

And so they all trooped out on to the stoop, where at least they had the benefit of the starlight. Then, from their various saddlebags, they produced several bottles of red-eye. Not possessing any mugs, they proceeded to drink the fiery liquid straight from the bottle.

Since Kitty was not carrying any whiskey, Wolf Brennan kindly shared his bottle with her. She, however, drank sparingly, for she had formed a plan and needed to have her wits about her if she was to pull it off.

As the evening wore on, the outlaws grew very merry. Old exploits were recounted, past successes exaggerated and a multitude of colourful jokes, most of which were pretty risque, related. No allowance was made for Kitty's presence. She was, after all, a sporting woman and, they assumed, used to such talk.

It was almost midnight when the first of the outlaws passed out. Legend has it that redskins do not have a head for strong liquor. Blue Duck confirmed this belief by falling off the stoop and stretching out on the ground beside the hitching-rail, face-downwards in a pile of horse dung, completely comatose.

At this point, the others decided it was time to retire for the night, and they all stumbled back inside the ranch house.

Very drunk and barely conscious, the Doyle brothers threw themselves down beside their saddles, which they used in place of pillows, and, hastily dragging blankets from their saddle-bags, draped these round themselves and promptly fell into a deep, alcohol-induced sleep.

Red Dawson fumbled about in the semi-darkness of the cabin until he found his saddle, and then proceeded to follow the example set him by the two brothers. Fred Carter, however, had other ideas. He staggered across the room and grabbed hold of Kitty.

'Let'sh you'n me have ourshelves a li'l fun,' he slurred.

'I don't think so.'

'Aw, c'mon!'

As Carter slid a horny hand inside the girl's cleavage and enveloped one of her full, ripe breasts, Kitty half-turned and dealt him a resounding slap across the cheek. The outlaw cried out and tottered backwards. At which point, Wolf Brennan stepped forward and caught him with a stiff uppercut to the jaw. The force of this blow lifted Carter clean off his feet and sent him crashing to the floor, where he lay senseless. As well as having a throbbing head in the morning, Fred Carter was now sure to be nursing a very painful jaw.

'Thanks,' said Kitty gratefully.

'My pleasure,' replied Brennan and, bending down, he picked up his saddle. 'I figure mebbe we should retire to the privacy of one of these here bedrooms,' he said.

'We? What *have* you in mind?' murmured Kitty in a most seductive whisper.

'I'm lookin' to tumble you, Miss O'Hara,' he growled.

'Why, I reckon I'd like that, Mr Brennan,' she murmured, as she snuggled up to him.

Carrying the saddle and saddle-bags in one hand and with the other gently squeezing the redhead's shoulder, Wolf Brennan guided her across the dark room towards the nearest bedroom. Kitty turned the handle and pushed open the door. Then, once they were inside, Brennan threw down both saddle and saddlebags and swept her up into his arms. The alcohol had inflamed the outlaw's desire and he kissed and caressed her with increasing intensity. Kitty responded passionately and soon they were tearing off each other's clothes in wild abandonment.

Eventually, stark naked and with their limbs entwined, they sank to the floor. There Wolf Brennan rained kisses in quick succession upon Kitty's face, neck, shoulders and breasts. Then he began to press his lips to her soft, white belly. Kitty moaned with pleasure, her legs parted and the outlaw swiftly mounted her. A frantic bout of lovemaking followed, culminating in their simultaneously reaching a wholly satisfying and sensational climax.

Immediately afterwards, the alcohol, which had helped fire Brennan's libido, affected him in quite another way. His passions satiated, he suddenly collapsed into a drunken stupor.

Kitty smiled. She slid from under the slumbering outlaw and pulled blankets from his saddle-bags. She covered both him and herself and, lying down beside him, composed herself for sleep.

Her plan was simple. She dared not attempt to flee during the hours of darkness, for she feared she would simply get lost. But, as soon as the sun began to show above the horizon, she intended to be off. Although she was not entirely sure where the horse-ranch was situated, she had taken note of the position of the sun and reckoned that, should she strike out in a north-easterly direction, she would eventually reach the main trail to Dallas at a point some miles north of Cactus City.

In the meantime, Kitty needed to snatch a few hours' rest. And, although she slept but fitfully, the redhead did indeed feel comparatively rested when the first faint rays of sunlight presently filtered through the bedroom window.

Immediately, Kitty slipped from beneath the blanket. She noted, with some satisfaction, that her erstwhile lover continued to sleep on.

Both her own and Wolf Brennan's clothes lay scattered across the floor, where they had been dropped. Kitty carefully separated them. But, instead of dressing in her own clothes, she began to pull on the outlaw's. The shirt and levis were both much too long for her, so she was forced to roll up the shirt-sleeves and the bottoms of the levis. Then she pulled on Brennan's leather jacket, from the sleeves of which her finger-tips only just protruded. The jacket, being rather too large in every way, perfectly disguised her figure. Her full, ripe breasts were quite undetectable beneath it.

The outlaw's low-crowned black Stetson was, in contrast, almost an exact fit. He had a narrow head, not much larger than Kitty's, and her thick, luxuriant red tresses, when tucked up inside, rendered the hat as though actually made for her.

Next, Kitty checked the inside pockets of Wolf Brennan's leather jacket. To her delight, she found the magnificent diamond necklace, which he had taken from Lo-Lo McCoy, together with a large wad of five and ten dollar bills. These bills he had evidently brought with him prior to the hold-up in Coyote Gulch, since he had taken none of the banknotes stolen there by the gang. Quickly, Kitty returned both the necklace and the banknotes to the inside jacket pockets and, picking up Brennan's boots, tiptoed across the bedroom floor to the door. She quietly opened it and slipped outside.

Despite the early morning gloom, Kitty could just about make out the sleeping forms of the four desperadoes stretched out in the ranch house's main chamber. Carefully, she skirted them and made her way to the front door. She opened this with the same care she had employed when opening the bedroom door. Then she stepped out into the cool morning air and placed the boots down on the stoop. Summoning up her courage, the redhead turned and went back into the building. A few moments later, she was back on the stoop, this time in possession of Wolf Brennan's saddle and saddle-bags, which now contained her previously discarded dress, undergarments, stockings and shoes.

Skirting the still comatose Blue Duck, Kitty carried all these items, including the boots, round to the small paddock at the rear of the ranch house. She paused at the well, where she proceeded to fill the water-flask she had filched off Brennan, and to wash the remains of her make-up from her face.

A part of her plan was to pass herself off as a fresh-faced youth, at least until she reached Dallas. Should Wolf Brennan, when he awoke, decide to pursue her, he would naturally enquire of those he passed on the trail whether they had seen a red-headed young woman in a dark-green dress, not a black-clad youth. And, anyway, he would surely have to delay any such pursuit until one of his gang had fetched him a fresh set of clothes. Since this would entail a ride to and from the nearest township, it could take several hours before he was ready to set forth.

Her ablutions completed, Kitty picked one of the seven horses at random. She thought it was the one she had ridden on the previous day, but could not be sure. Hastily, she swung the saddle up on to its back and then tightened the girth. Next she stepped into Wolf Brennan's boots, which, as she had expected, proved to be rather too big for her small feet. She placed her left foot in the near-side stirrup and then heaved herself up into the saddle. Bending down low, she held on tightly to the right boot while, at the same time, she placed her right foot into the other stirrup. Finally, she took hold of the reins.

'OK, boy,' she whispered into the animal's ear. 'Let's go!'

So befuddled by drink were the outlaws that not one of them was roused from his sleep by the sound of the horse's hoofs, as Kitty departed in what she hoped to be the direction of Dallas. She left the immediate vicinity of the ranch house at a quiet trot, waiting until she was several hundred yards away before speeding up into a full-blooded gallop.

Two hours passed. Then a bleary-eyed Wolf Brennan stirred and slowly came to his senses. As his recollection of the previous night came to mind, he turned beneath his blanket and stretched out an arm, intending to embrace his erstwhile lover. But the redhead was no longer beside him. He opened his eyes and peered round the bedroom. Of Kitty O'Hara there was no sign. For a moment, he was too dumbfounded to move. Then he scrambled to his feet and began to take stock.

His saddle and saddle-bags were missing. Brennan was pretty sure that Kitty had left hers in the ranch house's main chamber. However, he was just as certain that he had brought his into the bedroom. And where in tarnation were his and Kitty's clothes, he asked himself? Apart from the blankets, all that remained in the room were his Remington, holster and gun-belt, and his undergarments, which he had torn off in the course of their lovemaking. He hurriedly pulled on these combinations and strapped on his gun. Then he headed towards the open bedroom door and stepped into the living-room. As he did so, Fred Carter and Red Dawson woke up and stared open-eyed with wonder at their leader.

'What the hell?' exclaimed Carter, as he nursed his swollen jaw.

'Yeah, why are you standin' there in your

underclothes, Wolf?' enquired Dawson.

' 'Cause that goddamn red-headed whore has made off with the rest of my clothes!' roared Brennan, his face purple with rage and his black eyes glittering furiously.

'What . . . what's that?' cried Pat Doyle, as he, too, woke up.

His brother also emerged from his slumbers and slowly sat up.

'What's goin' on?' demanded Danny Doyle.

'Miss Kitty O'Hara has hightailed it outa here,' replied Carter. 'Takin' Wolf's clothes with her,' he added, laughing.

And the wallet, containing all of my money and that fancy diamond necklace, thought Brennan bleakly. Aloud, he said, 'Mebbe she ain't left yet? She could still be saddlin' up.'

He picked up his Colt Hartford rifle from where he had left it, and dashed outside. Passing a by-now-conscious Blue Duck, he headed round the ranch house in the direction of the paddock. And, as he ran, he scoured the surrounding prairie. But of the redhead there was no sign. Nor was she still in the paddock. Only six horses remained hobbled there. Brennan noted with some relief that his steed was among them. He sighed heavily and turned and slowly made his way back to the front of the ranch house.

As their erstwhile chief approached the stoop, his

five confederates clattered down the steps. They were each carrying their saddles and other equipment, and both the Doyle brothers had drawn their revolvers. The two Irish-Americans pointed their weapons at Wolf Brennan.

'What the blue blazes—?' he began.

'Drop that rifle an' unbuckle your gun-belt, then drop the revolver down beside the rifle,' said Pat Doyle.

'Or else?'

'Or else we shoot you dead,' said Danny Doyle.

Wolf Brennan glared at the five desperadoes, but made no move to do as he was bid.

'It's like this, Wolf,' explained Fred Carter. 'You are needin' some clothes. You cain't hardly ride into town in your undergarments.'

'So?'

'So, we figured that you'd likely reckon to shoot one of us an' take *his* clothes. Wa'al, that ain't gonna happen. You jest lay down your arms like Pat told you to.'

'Yeah, or me an' Danny'll fill you full o' lead. You better believe it.'

Wolf Brennan did believe it. Reluctantly, he complied. Then, when he had laid down his Remington and the Colt Hartford, Pat Doyle prodded him with his revolver and growled, 'OK. Now you can accompany us to the paddock.'

'Look here, how's about one of you fellers fetchin' me some clothes from the nearest township? That'll be—'

'Never mind where that'll be. We ain't fetchin' you no clothes, Wolf. We're outa here for good,' said Carter.

'For old times' sake?'

'Forgit it.'

The outlaws headed for the paddock, Brennan still protesting. And, while Pat Doyle kept his gun trained on their one-time chief, the others saddled and mounted their horses. Then Danny aimed *his* gun at Brennan and his brother saddled and mounted *his* horse.

'So long, Wolf. Been nice knowin' you,' said Fred Carter ironically.

The others laughed and followed Carter out of the paddock.

'Damn you all to hell!' cried Brennan, as they rode off.

Cursing furiously, he turned and ran back towards the front of the ranch house, where he had laid down his weapons. He snatched up the Colt Hartford and raised the stock to his shoulder. However, he was too late. His erstwhile companions had split up and were riding across the plain in different directions. And they were already out of range of the rifle. Nevertheless, he fired a couple of shots after them, but to no effect.

Still fuming, Brennan stepped into the house, retrieved Kitty's saddle and saddle-bags and then trudged back to the paddock. A few minutes later, he was mounted on his horse and riding off in the direction of Dallas. He figured that Kitty probably hadn't changed her plans to catch a train there. And he was determined to wreak vengeance upon the redhead and, at the same time, win back the diamond necklace.

SEVEN

At about the same time that Kitty O'Hara was dressing herself in Wolf Brennan's clothes, Jack Stone and Captain Johnnie Tranter were preparing to depart outside Flinder's Hotel. Matt Lewis stood on the stoop, watching them mount their horses.

'I really do appreciate this, Mr Stone,' he said. 'If you can track down them outlaws an' lead a posse to their hide-out, mebbe, jest mebbe, I'll git back that diamond necklace.'

'We'll do our best,' said Stone.

'Sure will,' averred Tranter.

'Wa'al, I'll take the next stage to Dallas an' await you there. If you don't find Wolf Brennan, I guess I'll have to break the bad news to Mr Pinkerton an' to the Widow Worthing's niece.' Lewis pulled a wry face. 'That ain't somethin' I'm lookin' forward to,' he confessed.

'See you in Dallas,' said Stone, and, without more ado, he turned the gelding's head and set off at a canter down Main Street.

Johnnie Tranter swiftly followed. He could scarcely contain his impatience. But it was Kitty O'Hara, not the Wolf Brennan gang, whom he was eager to capture.

They crossed the town limits and broke into a gallop. Ahead of them the trail stretched all the way back to Coyote Gulch and beyond. By dint of hard riding they reached the scene of the hold-up in a little under the hour.

Once there, the Kentuckian promptly dismounted and pored over the various tracks left in the dirt. He carefully examined the prints of the horses' hoofs, for he needed to distinguish between those leading into the gulch and those heading out of it. When he was quite satisfied, he climbed back into the saddle.

'OK,' he cried. 'Let's go!'

For the most part, the outlaws' tracks were fairly easy to follow. However, there were several lengthy stony tracts where Stone's tracking skills were tested to the full. Certainly, Tranter admitted to himself, he would almost certainly have lost them at these points. But Stone did not lose them. And, upon entering a small valley near the Trinity River, some time towards the middle of the morning, they came upon the deserted ranch house, where Wolf Brennan and his gang had spent the night. The lack of any horses in the vicinity of the cabin told them that their quarry had fled the scene.

'Goddammit!' ejaculated Tranter. 'They've gone!'

'So it would seem,' said Stone.

'You don't seem surprised.'

'No. Are you?'

'Wa'al, I had hoped—'

'Yeah. Anyhow, let's take a look around.'

The Kentuckian rode up to the ranch house, dismounted and tethered his bay gelding to the hitching-rail. Then he clattered up the short flight of wooden steps on to the stoop and went inside. Johnnie Tranter quickly followed. But the only traces of the outlaws' stay were a few empty whiskey bottles.

'So, what now?' demanded the disgruntled Texas Ranger.

'We see if we can pick up their trail, figure out where they're headed,' replied Stone.

'OK.'

The two men left the ranch house and walked round to the small paddock at the rear. Here it was plain to Johnnie Tranter that the desperadoes had split up, for there were clear tracks in the dirt indicating that they had gone their separate ways. He swore angrily.

'Who are we after?' asked Stone. 'Wolf Brennan or

Miss Kitty O'Hara?'

'I guess you're after Brennan. As for me, I'm commissioned to bring in the woman,' said Tranter.

'I'm afraid, Cap'n, there's no way of tellin' which are their partickler tracks.'

'No.'

'Miss O'Hara was on the stage bound for Dallas.'

'Yup.'

'So, mebbe that's where she's still headed for?'

'Could be.' Tranter's eyes glinted. The redhead was evidently trying to put as much distance as she could between herself and Double Drop. Well, once in Dallas, she could take a northbound train and, in a day or two, be in Chicago, or New York, or some other big city. That, he reckoned, had been her plan when she boarded the stage back in Double Drop. However, scared that her pursuers might overtake her in Coyote Gulch, she had thrown in her lot with the Brennan gang. But now what was more likely than that she should have resumed her journey to Dallas? 'Guess I'll head in that direction,' he said. 'What about you, Mr Stone?'

'Considerin' I ain't got no clue as to which set of tracks belongs to Wolf Brennan, I reckon I'll ride with you an' report back to Mr Lewis.'

'Do we need to retrace our steps to Coyote Gulch?'

'I don't think so. I figure we can find our way to Dallas from here.'

'If'n you're sure?' said Tranter, for he had no wish that they should waste time through getting lost.

'Pretty darned sure. Come on. Let's ride.'

The Kentuckian quickly turned and left the paddock. Johnnie Tranter decided to trust to the other's plainsman skills. Consequently, both he and Stone were in the saddle and galloping off across the plain within a couple of minutes of leaving the paddock.

They rode hard and fast. Stone was keen to report to Matt Lewis and then head southwards, with the hope that he still might reach San Antonio in time to join the annual cattle drive up the Goodnight-Loving Trail. Tranter, on the other hand, was determined that Kitty O'Hara should not escape him. He was riding the vengeance trail with murder in his heart. Both, therefore, had good reason to reach their destination with all possible speed.

The hours passed and it was late morning before they eventually reached the main north-south trail. Stone smiled grimly. He reckoned it would be late afternoon before they arrived in Dallas.

'This here's the trail we want,' he informed his companion. 'But we got a ways to go yet.'

'Let's hope we git to Dallas in time,' growled Tranter. 'If that whore—'

'Miss O'Hara cain't be more'n a few hours ahead of us.'

'Time enough to catch a train outa there 'fore we arrive.'

'Depends. There ain't that many trains leavin' Dallas in a day. Could be you'll catch her 'fore she can board one.'

'I pray you're right, Mr Stone.'

The Texas Ranger took the lead as the pair rode hell-for-leather northwards.

While Jack Stone and Johnnie Tranter were joining the trail, Wolf Brennan was way ahead of them, only ten miles short of Dallas. He had not dared follow the main route, dressed as he was in only his undergarments. Instead, he had kept himself hidden amongst the sagebrush, riding a parallel course. Now, with Dallas less than an hour away, the outlaw began to review his situation.

If his guess was correct, Kitty should be fairly easy to find in Dallas. That presupposed, of course, that the redhead hadn't already caught a train out of town by the time he got there. Brennan consoled himself with the thought that there were not too many trains heading north from Dallas. He prayed that Kitty would have missed all of that day's departures and so would be obliged to wait for the first train to leave on the following morning.

However, in order to search for and find Kitty, he would need to enter the town and, he reflected wryly, he could scarcely do so in his present state of undress. What he required was a set of clothes: hat, shirt, vest, trousers, boots; the lot. Even had Kitty not taken all his money, the outlaw would have been in no position to go shopping for these articles. Therefore, he must obtain them in some other way.

Wolf Brennan left his parallel course and veered off towards the trail. He had observed that half a mile ahead it wound its way northwards through a narrow gulch. There was nobody in sight as he emerged from the sagebrush and cantered on to the trail. He did not, however, ride on into the gulch. Instead, he urged his horse up a steep, twisting path that led to the bluffs overlooking the gulch's western perimeter. Upon reaching the top, he quickly dismounted and crouched down behind a tumble of boulders. From there he had a clear view of the trail in both directions.

To the south, as far as the eye could see, the trail was completely deserted. Brennan scowled and turned his attention northwards. The same. Muttering a curse, the outlaw told himself that he must be patient.

A southbound stagecoach passed through the gulch shortly before noon. Wolf Brennan let it go. He could easily have taken out the driver and his guard, but the passengers, whom he would also have had to dispose of, were an unknown quantity. Who were they? How many of them were there? And, most important of all, were they armed? Without a gang at his back, Brennan dared not tackle the stage. And, so, he settled down again and resumed his vigil.

It was mid-afternoon when a small cloud of dust suddenly appeared on the northern horizon. The outlaw watched it proceed slowly, yet inexorably, towards him. Then, when it was a little less than a mile distant, Brennan saw that it was a buckboard drawn by two horses, and that two men were sitting on its box. His scowl was replaced by a cruel smile.

Wolf Brennan rose and drew his Colt Hartford revolving rifle from the saddle-boot. He carefully replaced the bullets, which he had expended earlier at the deserted ranch house. Then he crouched down again to await the buckboard's arrival in the gulch.

Both the driver of the buckboard and his companion were quite oblivious of the fate that lay in store for them. They were chatting merrily, for they had been in town to purchase provisions and, while doing so, had availed themselves of the opportunity to quaff a few beers. Now they were on their way back to their ranch.

The driver of the buckboard was Ronnie Rogers, a tall, lean, lantern-jawed Texan. He owned the ranch to which they were headed. He had taken along short, fat, grey-haired Hank Laverty, since the latter, in his post as cook, knew what to buy and how much. At least, that was the rancher's reasoning. Anyway, Ronnie Rogers enjoyed the other's company, since the cook was an amiable and humorous character, who seemed to have a never-ending fund of jokes and comical anecdotes.

Indeed, Hank Laverty was in the middle of relating a particularly convoluted tale when the buckboard, having earlier rattled into the gulch, now reached a point directly beneath Wolf Brennan's hiding place. The cook never completed his story. Brennan's first shot struck his employer just above the right ear. The slug entered Ronnie Rogers' skull, ripped through his brain and exited out of his left ear. As he slumped sideways against the cook, the rancher let go of the horses' reins. The animals panicked and took off at a rare gallop, and Hank Laverty, in attempting to grab hold of the reins, lost his balance and toppled forwards off the box and beneath the runaway cart.

Wolf Brennan rose from behind the tumble of boulders and watched as the buckboard careered along the floor of the gulch and disappeared round a bend. Brennan observed the two men sprawled beneath him on the trail. Ronnie Rogers lay motionless, blood and brains oozing from his shattered skull. Hank Laverty, meanwhile, struggled to rise. One of the buckboard's wheels had passed over his leg, breaking his thigh. As he tried to move, he screamed with pain.

The outlaw raised the rifle to his shoulder, took aim and fired a second and final shot. It struck the cook in the neck, severing his jugular and causing a fountain of crimson to spout forth. Brennan smiled grimly. He reckoned that, by the time he reached the two men, the second would be stone dead like the first.

Brennan was quite right. The rancher and the cook lay stretched out lifeless upon the trail. Brennan eyed them both speculatively. Of the two, Ronnie Rogers most resembled himself. In fact, in height and build, they were almost identical. He grinned.

It took him a few minutes to relieve Ronnie Rogers of his clothing. The shirt, vest and denim pants fitted nigh perfectly, while the boots proved rather too tight a fit. Brennan removed these and tried on the cook's boots. To his surprise and delight, these were almost exactly his size.

Lastly, the outlaw picked up Rogers's wide-brimmed grey Stetson and Laverty's ancient brown derby hat. Both were liberally splattered with blood, as were the cook's upper garments. Brennan tried on both hats for size. Neither precisely fitted, the Stetson being much too large and the derby hat a little too small. Brennan chose the latter, adding a few extra dents to the ancient headpiece, as he stretched it in an effort to make it fit. Using some spiky tabosa grass from the side of the trail, he scrubbed off as much of the cook's blood as he was able. Then he slapped the hat on his head at a rakish angle and proceeded to mount his horse.

It was at the northern end of the gulch that Brennan observed a narrow stream trickling down one of its steep, rocky sides and into a small, shallow pond. Immediately, he pulled up his horse and dismounted. He went over to the pond and dipped his hat into the water. It took but a few minutes to wash all trace of blood from the hat, although, when he had completed this task, the surface of the pond was left a delicate shade of pink.

Wolf Brennan once again climbed into the saddle. He carried the hat in his left hand, intending to wait until it had dried out before replacing it on his head.

Ahead of him the trail wound its way across the plain in the direction of Dallas. The outlaw urged the horse into a gallop. Now that he was fully clothed, he felt confident that he could ride into town without rousing anyone's curiosity or suspicion. His features hardened into a look of fierce determination as he rode swiftly towards his goal. Would he arrive in Dallas in time to catch Kitty O'Hara before she could board a train and vanish? Assuming, of course, that that was still her plan? He brushed aside any thought that he might have guessed wrongly, and persevered with his fast and furious ride northwards.

EIGHT

At about the same time that Wolf Brennan was
watching his unsuspecting victims enter the gulch,
Kitty O'Hara was fast approaching the outskirts of
Dallas. She had passed several fellow travellers on her
ride north and, as far as she was aware, none had
penetrated her disguise. However, she feared that
she would not pass close inspection.

Consequently, she needed some place where she
could change back into her normal clothes. Kitty
knew the very spot. On the edge of town was a small
bordello, known as Mademoiselle Fifi's. It was here
that the redhead made for.

On her arrival, she dismounted and tied her horse
to the hitching-rail outside the bordello. Then she
grabbed hold of the saddle-bags and carried them
into the building. Once inside, Kitty found herself in

a small, dimly-lit antechamber. There were several red satin-covered chairs and a couple of settees scattered about this room. One large, rather tarnished mirror dominated the far wall and the place reeked of cheap perfumes. Two scantily-clad young women were sitting on one of the settees, chattering and giggling together. On the other an elderly, grey-haired gentleman was talking to a plump young blonde. It seemed to Kitty that they were conducting some kind of negotiation. As she closed the front door behind her, the man and the young woman concluded their conversation, rose and walked arm-in-arm through an arch leading, Kitty guessed, through to the bordello's bedchambers.

The pair had no sooner vanished than a small, attractive brunette, attired in a tight-fitting, low-cut black silk gown, stepped out through the same arch. She had a pair of bright blue eyes and a lively expression on her smiling face. The dim light and her carefully applied make-up conspired to make her look a deal younger than her forty-two years. Mademoiselle Fifi was the proprietor of the bordello and, although she affected a French accent for the benefit of her clientele, she hailed from Paris, Texas, rather than Paris, France. And her real name was Belinda Bunn.

'Hullo, Belinda,' said Kitty.

112

The brunette glanced sharply at the newcomer. Then, all at once, a glint of recognition showed in her bright blue eyes and she smiled widely.

'Hullo, Kitty,' she replied. 'What's with the weird get-up?'

'What's weird about it?'

'You know darned well what's weird about it. Them's men's clothes an' they don't fit you none too good neither.'

'No. Guess not.'

'You gonna explain?'

Kitty glanced towards the two girls chatting on the settee.

'Not here,' she murmured.

Belinda nodded.

'OK. You'd best come through.' She turned to the girls and said, 'In case you need me, I'm goin' through to my parlour.'

'Sure thing, Ma'moiselle,' replied the older of the two.

'We git any awkward customers, you bet we'll holler,' added the other with a grin.

Belinda smiled and led Kitty through the arch, down a short, narrow corridor and into her small, but pleasant, well-furnished parlour. She offered her visitor a glass of white wine and, when they had both sat down, she raised her glass and said, 'Nice to see you again. How long has it been?'

' 'Bout five years, I reckon,' said Kitty.

'Back in Wichita Falls?'

'That's right. We was both workin' at the Yellow Dog Saloon.'

Belinda pulled a wry face.

'Don't remind me,' she muttered.

'Wa'al, we've both moved on since then. An' you've done pretty well for yourself, *Ma'moiselle Fifi.*'

'I heard you had, too. Down south a ways in Double Drop.'

It was Kitty's turn to pull a wry face.

'Yeah. Till yesterday.'

'Oh! So, what happened yesterday?'

'It's a long story.'

'Which will no doubt explain your turnin' up here dressed in a man's clothes?'

'Yes.'

'Let's have it then.'

'OK.'

Kitty briefly and succinctly related to her friend all that had happened to her from the moment that Billy Tranter and she went upstairs in Double Drop's Longhorn Saloon.

'An' I'm here 'cause I need some place in which to change back into my own clothes 'fore I catch that northbound train I mentioned,' she concluded.

Belinda smiled sympathetically.

'You ain't gonna catch no northbound train

today. The last left Dallas, bout an hour back. You'll needs wait till the mornin',' she remarked. 'There's only the southbound train to Houston still due today.'

'That's OK, since I don't reckon nobody's gonna be lookin' for me here in Dallas.'

'No?'

'Why should they?'

'If'n you were spotted boardin' the stage back in Double Drop, then the peace officer there would've telegraphed his counterpart at the stage's next port of call, tellin' him to hold you until he could git a deppity to ride over an' pick you up.'

'That's true.'

'So, it was darned lucky the stage *was* held up. Otherwise you'd have got arrested the moment it rolled into Cactus City.'

'Mebbe? Dependin' on when Billy Tranter's body was found.'

'Anyway, the law will almost certainly have found out that you originally planned to ride the stage to Dallas.'

'They will also have found out that following the hold-up in Coyote Gulch, I lit out with Wolf Brennan an' his gang. So, why would they be lookin' for me here? Surely they'll assume I'm still somewhere out on the plains with them outlaws?'

'Good point.'

'I'll change here, then go book me a seat on the first train out tomorrow.'

'You know where you're headed?'

'Nope. As long as it's some place north, I don't care. Y'see, I ain't made up my mind whether I wanta settle in Chicago or in one of the East Coast cities. Like I said, I'll catch the first train out.'

'OK. You do that. Then come back here. I can put you up for the night.'

'No thanks, Belinda.'

'But why ever not?'

' 'Cause if I'm wrong an' the forces of law an' order do trace me here to Dallas, you could be in big trouble for takin' me in. Harbourin' someone wanted for murder is a serious offence.'

'Hell, that's a chance I'm prepared to take!'

'Wa'al, I ain't prepared to let you.' Kitty smiled gratefully at her friend. 'I got myself into this mess an' I'll git myself out of it. I only need two things from you: a place in which to change my clothes, an' for you to dispose of the hoss I tied up out front.'

'Oh, yeah! The hoss you took from them outlaws.'

'That's right. An' there's a saddle an' these here saddlebags to dispose of, too.'

'Put together, they could fetch quite a few dollars.'

'You're welcome to 'em, Belinda. I've got me some cash. Enough, I reckon, to set me up when eventually

116

I decide in which city I'm gonna settle. I'll change my name an' open either a florist's or a dress shop, an' start a new life.'

'You seem to have thought of everythin'.'

'Yes, I believe I have.'

'Wa'al, good luck, Kitty.'

'Thanks.'

Kitty opened the saddle-bags and pulled out her dark-green dress, cape and bonnet. These were somewhat rumpled, but she straightened them out as best she could. Then she pulled out a pair of stockings and some undergarments. When she had dressed herself in these last articles, she put on the dress, which Belinda helped her to button. Finally, she donned the cape and the bonnet and a pair of shoes. She stood before Belinda's mirror and eyed herself critically.

'Hmm. I do look a little crinkled,' she murmured.

'You've been travellin', so nobody will think anythin' of it,' retorted Belinda.

'No, I guess not.'

Kitty removed Wolf Brennan's wad of banknotes and the diamond necklace from the inside pockets of the outlaw's leather jacket.

'You wouldn't have a reticule you could spare, would you?' she asked, adding, 'I lost mine earlier.'

'Of course,' said Belinda.

The brunette quickly found one and Kitty

promptly transferred the money and the necklace into the small net bag.

'I'd best be goin',' she said.

The two women left Belinda's parlour and returned to the bordello's antechamber. It was now quite empty. Kitty guessed that the two young sporting women had had a couple of customers in their absence and were presently entertaining them. Then, just as Kitty was about to leave the premises, the door opened and a tall, elegant, middle-aged man, in a neat grey city-style three-piece suit and derby hat, stepped into the room. Belinda Bunn was immediately transformed into Mademoiselle Fifi.

'Ah, *bonjour. Monsieur*! You will be looking for some female company, *n'est-ce, pas?*' she trilled in a lilting pseudo-French accent.

'I surely am,' replied the man in grey.

'*Alors*, take a seat, *s'il vous plait.* I shall say farewell to my friend and then I shall be pleased to attend to your needs.'

'Thank you, Ma'moiselle.'

Smiling benignly, the gentleman sat down on one of the two settees. Belinda, meantime, stepped across the room and threw open the front door, which the gentleman had closed behind him. She and Kitty embraced on the threshold.

'*Au revoir, ma petite,*' murmured Belinda, although

both she and Kitty realized the word '*adieu*' would have been more appropriate.

She kissed Kitty on both cheeks. Kitty reciprocated and then they parted.

'Thanks for everything,' said Kitty, before turning on her heel and setting off down Main Street.

'The railway station is on the other side of town. Keep straight on down the street,' Belinda called after her friend. Then she stepped back inside the bordello and shut the door behind her.

Kitty smiled cheerfully. Things were looking up. A rosy future beckoned once she shook the dust of Texas off her feet. She walked briskly through the town, barely glancing at the shops and stores, although they were many and varied compared to what she had been accustomed to in Double Drop. Her aim was to catch the first train north to Kansas City in the morning and, while she didn't need to, she was anxious to purchase her ticket that very afternoon. It was silly, she knew, yet she could not relax properly until she had that ticket in her hand.

On arrival at the railway station, Kitty made straight for the booking office, a small wooden shack presided over by one Steve Baker. He was a youngish man, thin and gangly in his white shirt, black vest, trousers and shoes and small, round railwayman's cap. And he was bored and anxiously awaiting the arrival of the Houston-bound train so that, upon its departure, he might lock up and go home.

At the sight of Kitty, however, he brightened up considerably.

'Afternoon, ma'am,' he said, with a smile. 'How may I help you?'

'Can you tell me the time of the next train to Kansas City?'

'You've missed the last one today. It left 'bout an hour ago.'

'I know. But what time does the first one leave tomorrow?'

'Eight o' clock, ma'am.'

'May I purchase my ticket now?'

'Of course.'

Steve Baker was used to travellers purchasing their tickets in advance, particularly for early morning departures. He continued to smile as he took the redhead's money and handed over her ticket.

'Thank you.' Kitty returned the clerk's smile and asked, 'Can you recommend a hotel where I may spend the night?'

'I certainly can,' he replied. 'The Railway Hotel is 'bout fifty yards back along Main Street. It ain't too expensive an' it's clean an' comfortable.'

'That sounds perfect. Wa'al, thanks so much for your help.'

'My pleasure, ma'am.'

Kitty left the station and retraced her steps as far as the Railway Hotel. It proved to be very busy, with the vast majority of its patrons being travellers who were either awaiting the train bound for Houston, or, like Kitty, the morning one to Kansas City. Nevertheless, she succeeded in engaging a room for the night. Then, once she had been to her room and attended to her toilet, she made her way downstairs to the hotel restaurant, where she consumed a hearty supper.

It was early evening and dark outside by the time Kitty finished her meal. The redhead felt replete and pleasantly drowsy. It had been a long and tiring day. Although some time before the hour at which she usually retired, Kitty headed for her bedroom. She slowly climbed the stairs and trudged down the narrow, dimly-lit passage to her room. Once inside, she breathed a sigh of relief. She would retire immediately to bed, for she needed to make a relatively early start in the morning. And she had no wish to miss her train.

A couple of hours after Kitty O'Hara had ridden up to Mademoiselle Fifi's door, Wolf Brennan rode across the town limits and into Dallas. He rode past the bordello, but failed to recognize the horse which Kitty had left hitched outside. Perhaps this was due to the fact that there were three other horses tethered to the rail. Business was brisk at Mademoiselle Fifi's.

The outlaw hoped that he had guessed correctly and that Kitty had indeed headed for Dallas in pursuance of her original plan. Consequently, he rode straight through the town to the railway station.

Since the Houston-bound train was not due for another quarter of an hour, Steve Baker was still at his post when Wolf Brennan rode up to the station. The outlaw dismounted and hurried into the booking office. At once, Steve Baker looked up.

'How may I help you, sir?' he enquired.

'Wa'al, it's like this: I'm lookin' for my cousin Kitty. She's on her way to Kansas City, where she intends visitin' her sister Mary. As I have a present for Mary, which I'd hoped Kitty would deliver for me, I jest pray I ain't missed her.'

'What does your cousin Kitty look like?'

'She's a fine-lookin' woman, 'bout the same age as myself. A redhead, an' I, er, expect she was wearin' green. Her favourite colour.'

The railway clerk smiled.

'She was here earlier,' he said. 'At least, a woman answerin' to that description was.'

'Are you sayin' that she's already on her way to Kansas City?'

'No. She missed the last train. She has booked a

122

seat on the first one out of Dallas tomorrow mornin'.'

'Heaven be praised!' Brennan raised his eyes to the skies and attempted to look pious, but was not entirely successful. 'Would you happen to know what her plans are for this evenin? I guess she'll need a room for the night?' he said.

'That's right an' I recommended that she stay at the Railway Hotel,' replied Baker.

'Thanks. I'll look for her there.'

Brennan left the booking-office, mounted his horse and trotted off, back along Main Street. He did not bother to ask Steve Baker for directions, since he had earlier observed a hotel in close proximity to the railway station and assumed this to be the Railway Hotel.

There were several horses hitched to the rail outside the hotel and, when the outlaw entered through the front door, he found the lobby to be bustling with customers. On either side of the lobby stood doors to the restaurant and the bar-room. Diners and drinkers were constantly passing in and out of both. There was also a queue of people in front of the reception desk at the far end of the lobby. As Brennan watched, a couple were handed a key by the desk clerk and, clutching their luggage, made their weary way upstairs. Mademoiselle Fifi's was not the only establishment in Dallas doing brisk business that evening.

Wolf Brennan had just started down the lobby in the direction of the reception desk when Kitty O'Hara suddenly emerged from the hotel restaurant. Unfortunately for Brennan, several of the hotel's clientele either stood or milled about between him and his quarry. And, before he could push his way through the crowd, the redhead was already heading upstairs. As he elbowed his way to the front of the queue at the reception desk, Kitty reached the head of the stairs, then turned into the passage on her right hand and vanished from sight.

'Here, whaddya think you're up to?' enquired a red-faced, middle-aged traveller, who was in the process of registering himself and his wife.

'Yeah, git to the back of the queue!' snarled a thin, hatchet-faced salesman from Chicago.

'If you are looking for a room, sir,' interjected the desk clerk, 'I'm afraid you are out of luck. When I've attended to these folks ahead of you, there won't be a single room left to rent.'

Wolf Brennan scowled darkly, then collected himself. He had no wish to become the centre of attention. He needed to keep a low profile until he could get to the redhead.

'Sorry, folks,' he muttered. 'Guess I'll try some other hotel.'

'If, when you leave, you turn left, you'll find

McCain's 'bout a hundred yards away on the opposite side of the street. It ain't at all bad,' the clerk informed him.

'Thanks,' said Brennan.

He turned abruptly on his heel and hurried out of the hotel. Once outside on the stoop, he paused and glanced towards the hotel's upper floor and the row of bedroom windows. Most rooms were lighted, and he caught glimpses of various occupants as they passed before the windows or stood there, closing their curtains. One who stepped across the room and pulled shut the curtains was Kitty. Brennan smiled and made a quick calculation as to the location of that particular bedchamber.

The outlaw was determined to retrieve the diamond necklace and the wad of banknotes which Kitty had stolen from him. But he realized the need to exercise both patience and caution. He must achieve that end without alerting the hotel's other guests and, in so doing, the forces of law and order.

His plan was a simple one. He would wait until later, when the lobby was likely to be deserted. Should the clerk still be at his desk, he would stick a gun in his ribs and force the man to accompany him upstairs. Then, once inside Kitty's bedroom, he would KO the clerk and either strangle or smother the redhead before recovering the necklace and the money.

Brennan checked the pocket of Ronnie Rogers's vest and found that he was in luck. The rancher had secreted a small wad of dollar bills inside the pocket. Sufficient to purchase a decent supper, he reckoned. Smiling quietly, Wolf Brennan continued along the sidewalk until he reached Ma Parker's Eating House. *This'll do nicely,* he thought, and went inside.

NINE

A late afternoon sun shone down upon the two riders as they cantered along the trail in the direction of Dallas. At Jack Stone's insistence, they had reduced their pace. Johnnie Tranter, eager to catch up with Kitty O'Hara, had been unwilling to reduce their gallop to a canter. However, the Kentuckian had quickly pointed out that, unless they did so, their horses would soon be exhausted and unable to carry them the few remaining miles to Dallas. Reluctantly, therefore, Tranter had agreed to the other's suggestion.

Ahead of them lay a narrow gulch. As they rode into this, Stone urged his bay gelding forward and into the lead. Then, upon rounding a bend, he suddenly cried out.

'Holy cow! What have we got here?' he yelled.

Johnnie Tranter rode up alongside the Kentuckian.

'What in blue blazes—?' he said.

Ronnie Rogers's buckboard occupied the centre of the trail, and then, one hundred yards further on round another bend, they came upon the corpses of Hank Laverty and the rancher. The latter, they observed, was clad only in his undergarments.

Stone reined in his gelding and dismounted. He gazed in astonishment at the rancher's body.

'Seems to have been an ambush. Some bushwhacker's done for both of 'em. But why strip this feller of his clothes?'

'Beats me,' confessed a puzzled Johnnie Tranter.

'It don't make no sense. Anyways, we'd best lay the bodies out on that buckboard an' take 'em into town,' said Stone.

'Hell no! That'll hold us up an'—' began Tranter.

Stone stared coldly at the Texas Ranger.

'What kinda lawman are you, for Chrissake?' he rasped. 'You proposin' to leave 'em for the coyotes an' the buzzards to feed off?'

'I don't see no coyotes nor buzzards.'

'Not yet, but they'll sure as hell come sniffin' round.'

'Mebbe before then some other traveller will—'

'Cap'n Tranter, we can spare time enough to do our Christian duty.'

Johnnie Tranter noted the look in the Kentuckian's eye and his flat, dogmatic tone of voice.

He was not to be gainsaid. The Texas Ranger shrugged his shoulders resignedly.

'OK. Let's git on with it then,' he growled.

In the event, it was the work of only a few minutes to lift and lay out the bodies of the rancher and the cook on the buckboard. Then Stone clambered aboard and took up the reins. He set the buckboard going, while, ahead of him, Tranter cantered on down the trail, leading the gelding by its bridle.

It was in this manner, and a little over an hour later, that they eventually reached Dallas. As most folk were at supper and the town was lit only by splashes of yellow light spilling out of doorways and windows, they proceeded through the town to the law office without arousing either comment or incident. Here they dismounted and, having hitched their horses to the rail outside, stepped up and into the office.

Inside they found Sheriff Neil Wayne smoking a cigar and drinking coffee in company with the Pinkerton agent, Matt Lewis, who had arrived earlier by stagecoach.

'Why, Mr Stone! Cap'n Tranter!' exclaimed Lewis, as he swung round in his chair and observed them enter. 'How'd you do? Did you catch up with that stinkin', no-account critter, Wolf Brennan?'

'First things first, Matt,' said Stone, and he turned to face the sheriff. 'We stumbled across a coupla corpses on the trail. They're outside, layin' on a buckboard. Their buckboard, I reckon.'

'Right. Let's go have a look,' said the sheriff.

Neil Wayne was a tall, heavily-built, beetle-browed man in his early forties. He had been county sheriff for ten years and, in that time, had built a reputation for being firm but fair. He led the way outside.

'Jeez!' he gasped, as he gazed down at the two corpses.

'You recognize 'em?' enquired Stone.

'Sure do. Ronnie Rogers owns a ranch 'bout fifteen miles south of here. That other feller was his cook.' Sheriff Wayne glanced at the piles of provisions down beside which the bodies had been laid. 'Don't look as though they was bushwhacked by no ordinary outlaw. Leastways, whoever it was didn't trouble to take either the buckboard or any of them provisions.'

'No, but he did steal Mr Rogers's clothes,' remarked Stone.

'Yeah. That's sure a mystery,' confessed the sheriff.

'D'you reckon there's mebbe a connection between this business an' your search for Wolf Brennan an' Kitty O'Hara?' enquired Lewis.

'Why should there be?' demanded Tranter.

'You tell me, Cap'n.'

'Does the sheriff know what Mr Stone an' I are doin' here in Dallas?'

'He does. I explained everythin' to him. So did you succeed in trackin' Wolf Brennan to his hideout?'

'Yeah.' Tranter went on to relate how he and the Kentuckian had found the abandoned ranch house where Wolf Brennan and his gang had holed up for the night. And he concluded by stating, 'They'd all gone their separate ways by the time we got there. We've no idea in which direction Wolf Brennan made off. We headed for Dallas 'cause Mr Stone wanted to report back to you an' I had a hunch that Kitty O'Hara might've stuck to her original plan, which was to make for here.'

'But why was Miss O'Hara so keen to come to Dallas?' enquired the sheriff.

'So that she could catch a train headin' north from here. An' I reckon she's still aimin' to do jest that.'

'Yeah. She's probably aimin' to lose herself in one of them big northern cities,' explained Stone.

'Hmm. That makes sense,' said Neil Wayne.

'She could already be onboard some northbound train,' muttered Tranter gloomily.

'If'n she ain't, she won't catch another till mornin',' said Wayne.

'No?'

'Nope. The last train departed 'bout half an hour ago, an' that was headin' south.'

'Then, how do I find out if someone answerin' to Kitty's description boarded a train earlier today?'

'I'll take you round to Steve Baker's place. You can ask him. He's the bookin' office clerk.'

'Won't he be at the railway station?'

'I told you. The last train's gone. Station's closed till mornin'.'

'I see.' Tranter favoured the lawman with a grateful smile. 'OK. Please lead on, Sheriff,' he said.

The four men left the law office. They did not have far to walk. Steve Baker's home stood in West Street, which intersected Main Street a mere fifty yards away. His one-storey frame house was the second they came to once they had turned the corner into the side street.

They found Baker at home with his wife and baby daughter. He had not long finished supper. Sheriff Neil Wayne introduced him to the others. Then Johnnie Tranter put the question: 'Mr Baker, did a red-haired woman in a dark-green dress buy a ticket from you earlier today? She'd be in her late thirties, but is still pretty darned attractive.'

Steve Baker smiled at the memory of her.

'Oh, yeah, Cap'n! I sold a ticket to the lady you describe.'

'When was that?'

'A coupla hours back, I s'pose.'

'An' which train did she catch? Where was it headed?'

'She didn't catch no train. Jest booked a seat on the one leavin' at eight o'clock tomorrow mornin' for Kansas City.'

Johnnie Tranter grinned broadly.

'We've got her!' he exclaimed.

Steve Baker stared in surprise at the Texas Ranger. He would never have suspected Kitty of being a fugitive from justice.

'What . . . what's she s'posed to have done, Cap'n?' he asked.

'The sheriff'll tell you some other time. But can *you* tell *me* whereabouts in town I'm likely to find her?'

'As a matter of fact, I can. I directed her to the Railway Hotel,' said the clerk.

'OK. Let's go.'

'One moment. There's somethin' else you oughta know.'

'What?'

'It may not be important, but a feller, claimin' to be her cousin, was askin' 'bout her a while back. He referred to her as Kitty.'

'Yeah. That's her name all right,' interposed Matt Lewis. 'Can you describe this feller?'

'He was dressed in Western garb. I figured him to be a cowboy, mebbe even a rancher. He was tall an' lean, an' I couldn't help noticin' that he had a scar runnin' down the right side of his face.'

'Goddammit!' exclaimed Lewis. 'That describes Wolf Brennan to a tee!'

'But Brennan was dressed all in black last time we saw him,' remarked Stone.

'Which explains that double murder out on the trail,' said Sheriff Neil Wayne. 'An' why Ronnie Rogers has been stripped down to his under-garments. Wolf Brennan needed to adopt a disguise before ridin' into Dallas.'

'I don't understand,' growled Stone. 'Miss O'Hara lit out with him an' his gang directly followin' that hold-up in Coyote Gulch. So, why in tarnation would he be pursuin' her now?'

'Mebbe we'll find out when we catch up with her,' said Lewis.

'Yeah. Let's git round to the Railway Hotel pronto. We better find her 'fore Wolf Brennan does,' stated the sheriff.

The four men promptly took their leave of the young railway clerk and hurried outside. Then, led by the sheriff, they pelted along the town's badly lit sidewalks in the direction of the hotel. And, just as they reached a spot in Main Street exactly opposite Ma Parker's Eating House, Wolf Brennan stepped outside. He had satisfied his appetite, and now intended to return to the Railway Hotel and check as to whether

134

its lobby remained full of guests or was deserted.

It was Jack Stone who observed and recognized the outlaw, illuminated as he was by the light spilling out of the entrance to Ma Parker's establishment. Stone immediately leapt down from the sidewalk on to the main thoroughfare and headed across the darkened street towards the eating house. His companions, meanwhile, stumbled to a halt.

'Hold it right there, Brennan!' cried Stone, brandishing his Frontier Model Colt.

'What the hell—?' Wolf Brennan whirled round and peered anxiously out into the darkness. No shaft of light shone upon the Kentuckian. He remained a dark figure looming up out of the gloaming. 'Who . . . who are you?' rasped the outlaw.

'The name's Stone. Jack Stone.'

'Oh, yeah, I've heard of you! Sometime lawman. You got quite a reputation.'

'Yup.'

'So, whaddya want?'

'I want you, Brennan.'

'You got the wrong man. My name ain't Brennan.'

'No?'

'No.'

'Wa'al, I'll take you in an' let one of your victims have a look at you. Reckon he'll identify you as Wolf Brennan, the outlaw responsible for the recent hold-up in Coyote Gulch.'

'You ain't takin' me nowhere.'

'Don't be a fool. I got my gun trained on you. So, jest pull yours outa its holster nice 'n' easy an' toss it on to the ground.'

Wolf Brennan laughed harshly, mirthlessly.

'You're makin' a big mistake, Mr Stone,' he protested.

'We'll see 'bout that. For now, throw down your gun.'

The outlaw sighed and shrugged his shoulders.

'OK. If 'n you insist, guess I ain't got no choice.'

By this time Stone stood a mere thirty feet away and Brennan could see him rather more clearly. He smiled and dropped his hand on to the butt of his Remington. But the smile was false. As soon as his fingers closed round the gun-handle, it vanished, to be replaced by an evil snarl, and the revolver cleared leather in one smooth lightning draw.

Stone had not been duped by the other's sudden capitulation. He fired before Wolf Brennan could bring the Remington to bear. Once – twice – thrice the Frontier Model Colt barked. The three slugs ripped into the outlaw's chest, knocking him backwards a good six feet. He hit the sidewalk with a sickening thud and lay quite still.

The Kentuckian climbed up on to the sidewalk and bent down beside the fallen outlaw. The sheriff, Johnnie Tranter and Matt Lewis gathered round.

Stone glanced up at them.

'Wa'al?' murmured Sheriff Neil Wayne.

'He's dead,' said Stone.

'Guess that'll save us the expense of a trial,' reflected Wayne philosophically.

'Guess it will,' said Stone.

The shooting had attracted a number of Dallas's citizenry, most of whom emerged from Ma Parker's Eating House. The sheriff quickly shooed them off, but not before he had sent one of them to fetch the town's mortician. While he was doing this, Matt Lewis dropped on to his knees beside the dead man and began a thorough search of his clothing. He had just completed this search and was scrambling to his feet when the sheriff turned his attention once more to the corpse.

'What are you lookin' for, Mr Lewis?' he enquired.

'Whaddya think, Sheriff? That goddam diamond necklace stolen from me durin' the hold-up. The last I saw of it, Wolf Brennan had it in his hand.'

'Of course.'

'He ain't got it now, though.'

'So, where d'you think it is?'

'I think, Sheriff, that Miss Kitty O'Hara has it.'

'You do?'

'Yeah. That would explain Wolf Brennan's presence here in Dallas.'

'You figure she stole it off him, Matt?' asked Stone.

'I do indeed.'

'Wa'al, let's git round to the Railway Hotel an' see if you're right,' rasped Johnnie Tranter impatiently.

'OK. Follow me,' said the sheriff.

The four men resumed their dash towards the hotel. Behind them, the dead man sprawled across the sidewalk, awaiting the arrival of the mortician. He was soon surrounded by the small crowd which had come back following the sheriff's departure.

The four hustled in through the hotel's front door. The lobby lay deserted except for the solitary figure of the clerk, standing behind his desk at its far end. He looked up as they approached.

' 'Evenin', Sheriff. 'Evenin', gents. What can I do for you?' he asked affably.

'You got a resident, a Miss O'Hara?' demanded the sheriff.

'Sure have,' said the clerk, smiling. 'A darned good-lookin' red-headed woman. We don't git many as peachy as—'

'OK, Joel. Jest take us to her room,' Sheriff Wayne interrupted him.

The clerk studied the faces of the four men confronting him. All of them were hard-eyed and grim-visaged. He concluded that now was not the time to engage them in idle conversation.

'This way, gents,' he murmured, and led the way upstairs.

At the head of the stairs they turned right. A narrow, dimly-lit passage faced them. The clerk entered this corridor and halted outside the second door on his right.

'This is it,' he said quietly.

'Thanks, Joel,' said Wayne. 'You can leave us now.'

'OK, Sheriff.'

As the clerk headed off downstairs, Sheriff Wayne rapped loudly on the bedroom door.

'You decent, Miss O'Hara?' he shouted.

'Who . . . who wants to know?' enquired a voice from within.

'Sheriff Neil Wayne,' replied the lawman.

There was a gasp followed by a short silence. Then, after a couple of minutes, the redhead called out, 'I'm decent, Sheriff. You may come in.'

'Thanks.'

The quartet, led by the sheriff, barged into the sparsely furnished room. Kitty was standing beside the bed and fastening a last few buttons on her dress. Her lovely green eyes widened with fear and the colour faded from her cheeks upon observing that one of the men facing her was Captain Johnnie Tranter. Although, unlike his late brother, he had not been an habitué of Double Drop's Longhorn Saloon, nevertheless, she had seen him about town and straight away recognized him. He was the first to speak.

'Thought you could murder Billy an' git away with it, did you?' he snarled angrily.

'It-it wasn't murder!' she gasped.

'No?'

'No! It was self-defence.'

'Wa'al, the cap'n is takin' you back to Double Drop to stand trial,' stated Sheriff Neil Wayne. 'It'll be up to a jury to determine which it was.'

'That's right,' rasped Tranter, his eyes filled with hatred and his face contorted into a vengeful sneer.

Stone viewed the Texas Ranger with some disquiet. Why, he wondered, was Tranter so full of malice against the redhead? What was the dead man to him?

'The dead man. Billy. Who was he?' he asked Tranter.

It was Kitty, however, who replied.

'Billy was *his* younger brother,' she said, pointing at the Texas Ranger.

'Is that so?' said Stone and, turning to Tranter, he remarked, 'You kept that kinda quiet.'

'I didn't think it was nobody's business but mine,' retorted Tranter.

'No?'

'Nope. All I'm concerned with is that Billy should git justice. That's why I asked Sheriff Dunn, back in Double Drop, if I could be the one to pursue the fugitive. I was scared she might give some lunkhead of a deppity the slip.'

'I don't s'pose for one moment that Sheriff Dunn's deppities are lunkheads,' drawled Wayne. 'However, I can appreciate your wantin' to be sure Miss O'Hara is brought to trial.'

'Yup. So, if 'n you can accommodate her overnight in one of your cells, Sheriff, I'll take her back to Double Drop first light tomorrow.'

'You figurin' on takin' the stage, Cap'n?' enquired Stone.

'No. I got Rangers' business I've neglected, so I wanta git back there as soon as possible. I'll hire another hoss an'—'

'I ain't ridin' no hoss!' protested Kitty.

'You came here on hossback,' snapped Tranter.

'Yeah, an' I've got one heck of a sore ass to prove it,' said the redhead.

'That's jest too bad!'

' 'Sides, I ain't dressed to ride no hoss.'

'You were wearin' them self-same clothes when you lit out with the Brennan gang, followin' the hold-up in Cactus Gulch,' the Kentuckian pointed out.

'That was only half the distance 'tween here an' Double Drop. An' a mighty uncomfortable ride it was,' said Kitty. 'Which is why I stole Wolf Brennan's duds when I sneaked outa his hideaway an' resumed my journey to Dallas.'

'You stole Wolf Brennan's clothes!' exclaimed Stone.

'I did. Apart from makin' for an easier ride, I figured that he would have to wait there until one of his gang could ride into the nearest town for replacements. An' that would pretty well ensure he didn't reach Dallas till I was long gone.'

'Wa'al, your li'l plan failed on the second count,' commented Sheriff Wayne.

'Whaddya mean? Wolf Brennan ain't here. He's—'

'Dead,' said the sheriff. 'Mr Stone shot him dead a few minutes back.'

'No!'

'Yes.' A wide grin split Wayne's rugged features. 'Hell, that means the sonofabitch must've ridden God knows how many miles either in his combinations or stark naked!' he chortled.

This happy thought brought forth guffaws of laughter from both Jack Stone and Matt Lewis. Only Johnnie Tranter failed to join in the general merriment.

'Which is why he shot those two fellers out on the trail an' took the clothes off one of 'em,' stated the Texas Ranger.

Kitty's bright green eyes opened wide in horror.

'Oh, no!' she cried. 'Did he really?'

'I'm afraid so,' said Wayne.

'Then I guess I'm responsible for their deaths!'

'Don't fret yourself on that score, Miss O'Hara,' said Stone. 'Even had Wolf Brennan not lost his clothes, he would've done what he did. Y'see, he daren't ride into Dallas dressed all in black, his usual attire, or he'd have risked bein' spotted straight away. No, he needed that feller's clothes as a disguise.'

'That's right,' added Wayne.

Matt Lewis watched the relief show in Kitty's face and then said quietly, 'His clothing wasn't the only thing you stole from Wolf Brennan, was it, Miss O'Hara?'

The redhead looked suddenly guilty and was quite unable to prevent herself from glancing at her reticule, which lay on her bedside table. Almost immediately, she averted her gaze, but she was too late. The Pinkerton man quickly crossed the room and, before she could protest, lifted the reticule off the table. He pulled on the draw-strings to open it, Then he up-ended it and a large wad of banknotes, a railway ticket and the missing diamond necklace dropped into his hand. He replaced the banknotes and the railway ticket inside the reticule, closed it and tossed it back on to the bedside table. Kitty straightaway picked it up and stuffed it into a secret pocket inside her dress.

'This is what I want,' said Lewis, holding the necklace aloft. He turned to the Kentuckian. 'Seems, Jack, that Mr Pinkerton's gonna be mighty pleased. I'll wire him tomorrow to make sure your wages an' a decent bonus are deposited at the Cattlemen's

Bank in San Antonio. It'll be there waitin' for you.'

'Fine.' Stone eyed the redhead and remarked, 'So, that's why Wolf Brennan pursued you all the way here. We guessed as much when Matt searched the sonofabitch's body an' couldn't find the necklace. Now he'll be able to return it to its rightful owner, the late Mrs Worthing's niece.'

'Sure will,' said Lewis happily.

'An' you,' Tranter addressed Kitty, 'will be ridin' back to Double Drop to stand trial for my brother's murder.'

'I tell you, I cain't ride no hoss. I—'

'If you don't wanta take the stage, Cap'n, you could hire a gig. That would solve your problem,' suggested Stone.

'Yeah. You can mebbe force Miss O'Hara to travel by hossback, but you sure as hell cain't force her to ride fast. An' she ain't gonna be in no great hurry to reach Double Drop,' said the sheriff, adding pointedly, 'I reckon you'd travel quicker by gig.'

Johnnie Tranter smiled grimly.

'You could be right,' he conceded. 'OK. I'll hire me a gig. I can always git one of my papa's hands to bring it back here when I'm finished with it.'

'Your papa owns a ranch?' asked Wayne.

'Yeah.' Tranter continued to smile grimly. 'Colonel James Tranter. One of the wealthiest men in Maxwell County,' he declaimed proudly.

The sheriff looked impressed, Stone and Lewis somewhat less so.

'So, that's settled then,' said Stone. 'Miss O'Hara spends the night in jail, then at first light you escort her back to Double Drop.'

'What about you, Jack?' said Matt Lewis. 'You still reckon you can reach San Antonio in time to join that cattle drive?'

'I think so. An' once you've handed over the diamond necklace to its owner what are your plans?'

'I head north for Chicago.' A huge grin split the young Pinkerton man's features and he declared, 'I cain't hardly wait to be home again.'

'Wa'al, let's git movin',' said Tranter sharply, whereupon he grabbed hold of Kitty and marched her out of the room. Sheriff Neil Wayne hurried after them.

'I dunno 'bout you, Matt,' said Stone, when the others had disappeared down the passage, 'but I guess I'll have me an early night. It's been one helluva day an' I also wanta leave town at first light.'

'That figures,' smiled Lewis. 'But hows about we have jest one for the road?'

Stone returned the other's smile.

'Why not?' he growled, and they headed off downstairs to the bar-room.

TEN

In the event, that night Jack Stone and Matt Lewis shared the last available room in nearby McCain's Hotel. They had retired early as planned, although, in fact, they had had two for the road.

As dawn was breaking they parted on the stoop outside the hotel.

'Goodbye, Jack. Thanks for all your help,' said Lewis.

'It was a pleasure. Good luck to you, Matt,' replied Stone.

'An' to you.'

The two men shook hands and immediately went their separate ways. The Pinkerton agent departed in search of the residence of the Widow Worthing's niece, while the Kentuckian headed for the livery stables to pick up his bay gelding.

Once he had saddled and mounted the gelding,

Stone rode along Main Street in the direction of the law office. As he approached it, Captain Johnnie Tranter appeared round the corner of East Street in a gig drawn by a dun-coloured mare. His black stallion was hitched to the rear of the gig and trotted along behind.

'I thought I might see you at the livery stables,' remarked Stone.

'You might have, if a friend of the sheriff hadn't offered to hire me this here gig,' replied Tranter.

'Nice-lookin' vehicle. An' that mare looks pretty mettlesome,' commented Stone.

'Yeah. Reckon both will serve to git me an' my prisoner safely back to Double Drop.'

'Should do.'

As Stone spoke, the door of the law office was flung open and Sheriff Neil Wayne stepped outside. He grasped Kitty O'Hara by the left arm.

'Here we are, Cap'n. She's all yours,' said the sheriff.

Tranter grinned and, producing a pair of handcuffs, approached the law office. He brandished the cuffs in front of the redhead's anxious gaze.

'Jest in case you try to escape,' he rasped.

'How . . . how can I possibly do that? You're armed an'—'

'Wa'al, I ain't takin' no chances.'

'Aw, c'mon, Cap'n, that surely ain't necessary?'

147

protested Stone.

'She's my prisoner an' therefore my responsibility. So, I'll decide what is, and what isn't, necessary,' retorted Tranter.

'Guess it's his call,' said the sheriff to the Kentuckian.

Stone shrugged his brawny shoulders and watched while the Texas Ranger dragged the girl's arms behind her back and handcuffed her wrists together. He did so none too gently, causing Kitty to grimace and cry out.

'OK. Let's lam outa here,' snapped Tranter. He turned and grasped the sheriff by the hand. 'Thanks, Sheriff,' he said.

Then he hastily bundled Kitty into the gig and clambered up beside her. He grabbed hold of the reins. Kitty, meantime, attempted to arrange herself into a comfortable sitting position, a move not helped by the fact that her hands were handcuffed behind her back. She glanced imploringly at the Kentuckian.

'I b'lieve you said you were headin' south?' she gasped.

'That's right,' replied Stone.

'Will you be ridin' with us as far as Double Drop?'

'I can do.'

'Oh, no!' said Tranter.

'Yes, please!' cried Kitty for, although she was

148

dreading her arrival and subsequent trial in Double Drop, she was dreading even more making the journey alone with Johnnie Tranter. She did not know exactly what she feared from him, but she had a presentiment that he had some truly evil plan in mind.

'There ain't no call for you to delay your arrival in San Antonio,' said Tranter to the Kentuckian. 'You spoke about gittin' there in time to enlist on some cattle drive. Wa'al, you'll sure as hell ride a lot faster if'n you don't wait for us. This gig cain't match the pace of your gelding no-how.'

'I s'pose not,' said Stone.

' 'Course not. An' I won't hear of you hangin' fire on our account.' The Texas Ranger leant towards the mounted Kentuckian and stretched out his hand. 'Goodbye, Mr Stone, an' thanks for everythin',' he said.

' 'Bye, Cap'n.'

'No! Don't go!' cried Kitty, but to no avail.

Stone turned the gelding's head and dug his heels into the animal's flanks. Then he cantered off southwards along Main Street. Ahead of him, the trail led across the plains, through Cactus City, Double Drop and several other small townships on the way to San Antonio.

The girl turned in desperation to the sheriff.

'Sheriff, couldn't you spare a deppity to ride along

with us?' she asked anxiously.

'Why in blue blazes would I do that? I'm sure the Cap'n is perfectly capable of escortin' you back to Double Drop,' said Wayne.

'I-I don't trust him. It was his brother I killed an', wa'al, it don't seem right that he should be the one who—'

'I'm only lookin' for Billy to git justice,' said Tranter. 'Hell, Sheriff, I'm a lawman like you, ain't I?'

'That's right.' Wayne turned to address Kitty. 'Sorry, miss,' he said, 'but I cain't see no good reason to grant your request. Therefore, I'll bid you farewell an' say only that I trust justice will be done.'

Thereupon, he bade Johnnie Tranter bon voyage and then stood and watched as the Texas Ranger flipped the reins and set the gig in motion. It promptly proceeded along Main Street in the wake of the recently departed Kentuckian.

Kitty was still protesting as they crossed the town limits and headed southwards. The handcuffs were chafing her wrists and, at the same time, making it difficult for her to maintain an upright position as the gig rattled at speed over the uneven surface of the trail. When she slipped sideways and bumped into Johnnie Tranter, he elbowed her sharply in the ribs. This caused her to topple in the opposite direction, and only with great difficulty did she prevent herself from falling out of the gig.

Eventually, after this had happened a dozen or more times, Kitty cried out, 'For pity's sake, won't you remove these danged cuffs?'

Tranter laughed harshly.

'You think I'm crazy?' he snarled. 'Like I said earlier, I ain't takin' no chances with you.'

'Then cuff my hands together in front of me. That way—'

'Shuddup!'

'But—'

'Shuddup!'

Tranter glowered at the redhead and cracked her hard across the mouth with the back of his left hand. The force of the blow split her lip and caused a trickle of blood to run down over her chin and drip on to the floor of the gig. She gasped with pain, but said nothing, for she had no wish to suffer a second blow.

The Texas Ranger smiled to himself and reverted his attention to the trail ahead.

The next few miles were completed in silence. Kitty was by now both thoroughly frightened and intimidated while, for the moment, Johnnie Tranter had nothing to say.

They had travelled approximately seven miles across the cactus-speckled plains when they spotted a low hill ahead of them. A narrow track branched eastwards off the main trail, skirted the foot of this

151

hill and disappeared between a stand of cottonwoods and the base of the hill.

Kitty expected that they would remain on the main trail and consequently pass by on the hill's western flank. However, Johnnie Tranter had a different idea. He took the left-hand fork and sent the gig rattling along the narrow track towards the cottonwoods.

'Hey, where in tarnation are we goin'?' cried Kitty. 'This ain't the way to Double Drop!'

'No, it ain't,' snapped Tranter.

'Then, where—?'

'Shuddup! You'll find out soon enough.'

Kitty opened her mouth to protest further, but caught Tranter's glare and hastily closed it again. She had no wish to provoke yet another slap across the face. So, for the second time that morning, she reluctantly held her tongue.

Presently, the gig passed round the base of the hill to a point where both the hill and the trees screened it from anyone travelling along the main Dallas-San Antonio trail. It was here that Tranter pulled hard upon the reins and brought the gig to a halt.

'Why-why are we stoppin'?' demanded a by now very frightened Kitty O'Hara.

'Why d'you think?' snarled Tranter.

'I-I don't know.'

'Guess.'

'No.'

'Scared to?'

'Er, mebbe I am,' she gasped nervously.

Johnnie Tranter emitted a harsh, mirthless laugh.

'Then I reckon I'd best tell you,' he said.

'Yes.'

'I've stopped here 'cause this is where I aim to avenge Billy's murder.'

'But-but why, for God's sake? If you're so sure it *was* murder, why not leave it to a jury in Double Drop to convict me?'

'If, as you claim, you acted in self-defence, why didn't you stay to clear your name?'

'I was afraid I'd be found guilty. Hell, your pa would've rigged that jury to make darned sure I was convicted!'

'You think so?'

'I do.'

'Papa surely exerts a lotta influence in Maxwell County, yet I don't believe he'd have succeeded in riggin' no jury.'

'No?'

'No. Y'see, Judge Jeremiah Jeffries is a high-minded, stiff-backed old bastard, who'd almost certainly dismiss anyone he considered to be biased. There'd be no jury-riggin' in his court.'

Kitty's face dropped and her eyes showed all too clearly the chagrin she felt. Had she realized that

Colonel Tranter could *not* have pressed the jury to find her guilty, she might well have stayed on in Double Drop, taken her chance and stood trial. 'Ain't that ironic?' she remarked. 'I fled Double Drop 'cause I was afraid I'd be found guilty, an' you ain't gonna take me back there 'cause you're afraid I *won't* be found guilty.'

'I'm jest makin' sure justice is done,' said Tranter.

'So, you're gonna be judge, jury *an'* executioner!'

'Sure am.'

'But it *was* self-defence! Billy refused to pay for my services an' tried to force hisself upon me. Then, when I resisted, he drew a knife an' threatened to cut me up real good. So, I shot him. I had absolutely no choice in the matter. It was him or me.'

'You lyin' slut! I don't b'lieve a goddam word. You murdered Billy in cold blood, reckoned you'd rob him an' lam outa town. How else d'you explain that wad of banknotes we found in your reticule?'

'I tell you, Billy didn't have no money. Those notes belonged to Wolf Brennan. I took 'em to replace my savin's, which he stole from me in Coyote Gulch.'

'Huh! A likely story.'

Tranter grabbed Kitty by the arm and dragged her down out of the gig. Then he threw her to the ground and walked to the rear of the gig, where his black stallion stood quietly waiting. He reached up into one of his saddlebags and brought out a length of coiled rope. At one end of the coil was a ready-made noose.

'I'm gonna hang you from that tree over there,' he informed her.

'No! No!'

'Yes. An' I promise you ain't gonna die easy. I'm gonna string you up an' leave you danglin'. There'll be no sudden drop. You will slowly choke to death.'

'You-you cain't do this! You're a peace officer. You—'

'Aw, suddup!'

Tranter took a couple of steps towards the prostrate redhead when a voice, seemingly out of nowhere, told him to back off. He stopped in mid-stride and turned his head to face the speaker. And there, standing amongst a tumble of boulders at the base of the hill, was none other than the Kentuckian, Jack Stone.

'What in blue blazes are you doin' here?' demanded Tranter.

'Preventin' a murder,' replied Stone.

'What murder, for Chris'sake?'

'The murder of Miss O'Hara.'

'This ain't gonna be no murder. It's simply an execution of justice.'

'Not in my book, it ain't.'

'How come you're here, anyway?'

'Put it down to instinct. I had a feelin' you didn't

intend handin' Miss O'Hara over to the authorities down in Double Drop. So, when I spotted this here track forkin' off the main trail, I had me a sudden presentiment. Consequently, I rode up to the top of the hill an' watched events. Eventually, you appeared along the trail. Then you turned off on to this track. At that point, I hobbled my hoss an' made my way back down the hill, all the while keepin' you in my sights.'

'I see. So, now what?'

'I suggest you mount that stallion of yourn an' ride off.'

'An' jest what do you intend doin'?'

'What you should've done, Cap'n. I intend escortin' Miss O'Hara back to Double Drop.'

'Over my dead body.'

'If necessary.'

Johnnie Tranter permitted himself a wintry smile. He had ridden the vengeance trail and he was not about to back down now. The death of his young brother would be avenged, or he would perish in the attempt.

Which is precisely what he did. Like all Texas Rangers, Johnnie Tranter was a darned good shot. But in a shoot-out he was no match for a gunfighter of Stone's calibre.

He was still smiling when suddenly Stone sprang into action, his Frontier Model Colt blazing. Tranter stood open-mouthed as the slugs ploughed into his chest. He had not even had time to pull his revolver clear of its holster before he was hit and knocked backwards several feet, the bullets smashing through his body and exiting out of his back in a stream of blood and splintered bone. By the time he hit the ground, his shirt front was stained crimson and he was already dead.

'Jeez! That was quick!' exclaimed Kitty.

'He wasn't gonna back down,' said Stone.

'No.'

Stone crouched down beside the dead man and fished a key out of his vest pocket. He crossed over to where Kitty lay and proceeded to unlock the handcuffs which held her. Kitty sat up and began to rub the circulation back into her wrists. Then, once she had achieved this, she scrambled to her feet.

'So, what now, Mr Stone?' she asked anxiously. 'Are you gonna take me back to Double Drop?'

'I don't think so.'

The redhead's heart gave a little skip and a relieved smile flitted across her pretty face.

'You believe, then, that when I killed Billy, I did so in self-defence?' she murmured.

'Yup,' said Stone. 'However, a jury might come to a different conclusion. Therefore, I don't feel we oughta put the matter to the test.'

'Oh, nor do I!' Kitty declared fervently. Then she

glanced at the bloodstained body of Johnnie Tranter. 'But what about him?' she asked.

'We'll drape him across the saddle of his hoss an' send the hoss trottin' along the trail back towards Dallas. Somebody's sure to stumble across 'em an' take 'em into town.'

'An' when they do, the sheriff will be lookin' to find out who shot him.'

'Wa'al, he can hardly suspect you. He was witness to your leavin' Dallas with your wrists handcuffed behind your back.'

'That's true.'

'So, I reckon your disappearance an' Cap'n Tranter's death will remain one of the great unsolved mysteries of the West.'

Kitty sighed. It seemed that her troubles were pretty much over. She pulled her reticule from the pocket hidden inside her dress. She opened it and peered at its contents.

'I guess you'll be resumin' your journey south?' she said.

'Yeah. An' what about you? Still aimin' to catch a train to Kansas City?'

Kitty flourished her ticket.

'This guarantees me a seat from Dallas. However, I daren't return there. If the sheriff spotted me—'

'That gig. Are you capable of drivin' it?'

'Oh, yes, Mr Stone! I certainly am.'

'Then why don't you head on back the way you jest came? Only make sure that you avoid Dallas. There's a fork on your left immediately 'fore you reach the town limits. This skirts the town an' joins up with the main trail a mile or so north of Dallas.'

Kitty's smile was truly beatific.

'I'll take that fork!' she cried delightedly.

'The next town along the trail is Greenville,' said Stone. 'You can board any of the Kansas City trains there.'

'Yes, though I'll need to purchase another train ticket,' said Kitty.

'Why should you need to do that?'

'Because it would seem odd me boardin' a train at Greenville when I purchased my ticket at Dallas. The ticket-collector would surely want some kinda explanation?'

The big Kentuckian shrugged his burly shoulders.

'So?'

'What would I tell him?'

Stone grinned broadly.

'You'll think of somethin',' he said.